THE LADY VANISHES

Rose gasped. "Leslie! Where is she? Mrs. Hanson, where is Leslie?"

"I don't know. I swear to God, I don't know. She was right here in the house when the lights went out. I could hear her upstairs. Then this gust of wind blew open the kitchen door. But I could hear water running. Well, I just took it for granted she was in the tub. Then the lights went out. After that, there was that *thing*—you know, the voice."

"But you said you heard her upstairs." Rose was no longer weak and trembling with fear. She was afraid, but she felt stronger, more able to cope.

"I did. I heard her scream bloody murder."

"Did you go upstairs?"

"Why, of course I went upstairs! Did you think I'd just let her stay up there all by herself in a bath-tub, not a light on in the house and ghosts stalking around trying to get in the windows and her screamin' like that?"

"Why did you say that, Mrs. Hanson, about ghosts trying to get in the windows?" Allan's voice was pleasant.

"Because there was this tapping sound on the outside of the house, that's why. All over, it seemed like. So I lit a candle and went right up. But she wasn't there. She just . . . well, there isn't any other way to say it. That girl just simply *disappeared!*"

WINTER ROSES

LORINDA HAGEN

LEISURE BOOKS ❧ NEW YORK CITY

Dedicated to Cora Williams

This is a work of fiction. Any resemblance to any person or persons living or dead is purely coincidental.

A LEISURE BOOK

Published by

Dorchester Publishing Co., Inc.
6 East 39th Street
New York, NY 10016

Printed in the United States of America

WINTER ROSES

I

The Volkswagen Bug was icy cold when Leslie Ellison left work that afternoon. Each breath she took clouded the windshield and within seconds a thin layer of ice crystals covered every glass surface. It would be a few minutes before the heater would make the interior of the car comfortable, but Leslie had never regretted her purchase. A Volkswagen was economical and the saleman had assured her it would go anywhere, any time, including the winter roads from Carson City, Nevada, where she worked, to the higher, mountainous drive required to get her home to Virginia City.

She remembered his words clearly when she put the key in the ignition and nothing happened. Frowning, she turned the key and pumped the accelerator. No welcome sound of an engine catching and holding as usual. Someone had once told her it was futile to grind away at the starter, and the feeble growl after a few more attempts made it clear she was in danger of running down the battery. The thin layer of ice on her windshield kept her from seeing anything very clearly, but she thought she saw a shadow float in front of her. But no, it was no one— merely a red glow which showed that the only other car in the parking lot, aside from hers, was backing out and driving away. Her feet were cold and her gloved hands felt frozen.

It was too late for her to go back to the office for help, because she had been the last one to leave. A State Senator had asked her to type a letter for him and drop it in the mail slot when she left. She did, but at the moment she wished she had asked him to stick around and mail it for himself. If she didn't freeze to death. The temperature was hovering near zero and the few flakes of snow that had begun to fall earlier in the afternoon had turned into a full-fledged blizzard.

She scraped a hole in the ice on the window and saw nothing but darkness, then glanced wistfully at the Governor's mansion, just barely visible beyond the State Building where she worked. According to her co-workers, the Governor and his wife were warm-hearted people and easy to relate to, but Leslie had been living in Nevada only a little more than three months and the idea of knocking on the door of the Governor's Mansion was appalling. Most of the time she managed to hide her native shyness by forcing herself to smile and look the world in the eye. She was nineteen, she reminded herself severely, capable of holding down an excellent job, and had even found the strength to break off her engagement just a day before the wedding, although at the time she was afraid it would kill her. Even so, the idea of going to the Governor for help brought on an attack of anxiety.

A dark shape loomed up at the side of her car. The moving figure was silhouetted against the pale lights in the parking area, and a pleasant voice called out, "Are you having car trouble?"

Leslie rolled down the window, overwhelmed with relief. "Mr. Holliday, I'm so glad to see you! I was about to get out and walk the eight or ten blocks to town."

The world-famous photographer shook his head. "You'd never make it, Miss Ellison. Move over and let me see if I can get it started for you."

Gratefully, Leslie climbed over the gearshift and flopped into the other seat, the cold penetrating through her heavy coat. "I thought everyone had left," she said through chattering teeth. She had met the photographer two days ago when her supervisor explained that Mr. Holliday was doing a picture story on Carson City. Later she had seen him engrossed in conversation with the Governor.

"I was waiting for people to move their cars away so I could get a shot of the Mansion from a distance," he said. He turned the key, but even the grinding sound had stopped. "I'm afraid the battery is dead. Where do you live, Miss Ellison? I'll take you home."

"Oh, no, that won't be necessary. I live in Virginia City, on top of a high hill a few miles outside of town. If you'll just be kind enough to take me to a taxi stand, I'd appreciate that."

"Nonsense. Virginia City isn't all that far away, and I'll enjoy the drive. This snow is beautiful, isn't it?"

"I'm afraid I don't appreciate it right now," she said as she got out of her Volkswagen. Their footsteps crunched in the snow as they made their way

9

around the building, and the wind that whipped around the corner made Leslie's eyes water. Shivering, she said, "Only a Volkswagen or a car with tire chains will be able to make it up the hill to my aunt's house, Mr. Holliday. And the taxis will have chains on by now."

His laugh was friendly as he handed her into the cab of what she took for a pick-up truck. When he was behind the wheel he explained that his four-wheel drive would go where other vehicles bogged down, and he insisted on taking her all the way home. "I'm from North Carolina, where people are friendly," he said as he pulled out of the traffic onto Route 79. "But I must say Nevada folk go out of their way to be hospitable. Were you born here, Miss Ellison?"

"No, I was born in San Francisco. In fact, I've lived here a very short time. I'm making my home with my aunt. It isn't far to Virginia City, but it seems like miles and miles when the weather is bad."

"While I'm in the vicinity, I intend to take some pictures of Virginia City, too. I've been so busy working on the Carson City story that I've not had a chance to do anything else. I understand the place is reeking with lore, and a great number of artists and writers are living there, that they've begun a regular colony."

"The town has been restored and it is picturesque. And of course there's a great deal of history and legend. But in the winter, most of the business places close down because the roads from Reno, where most of the tourists come from, are impassable. My aunt is a writer, but I don't know if there's an actual colony established in Virginia City or not.

She's Rose Winters, but she writes under the name of Rose Delamar, her maiden name."

Holliday's voice sounded pleased. "Of course. Rose Delamar is my favorite mystery writer."

The four-wheeler lurched to one side and for a sickening moment Leslie was afraid they were going to slide off the edge of the mountain. In the darkness, she closed her eyes and instinctively protected her face with her hands. By the time he had the vehicle under control, she was glad it was dark so he couldn't see the way she had reacted.

"Slippery as the devil," he commented. "Better fasten your safety belt."

"It's fastened," she said in a small voice.

Then she began to breathe easier because they were on a level stretch of road. She was almost hysterically grateful for the warmth of the heater, and the expert way Mr. Holliday handled the wheel. The windshield wipers were moving fast, but they weren't quite able to keep the snow from accumulating. As they climbed the grade, she saw that the road was covered with several inches of snow, much more than there had been when they first drove onto the highway. Another hill was coming up and she held her breath and hung on. Holliday kept a steady speed, didn't brake when the wheels slid, and Leslie expelled her breath gratefully when they crested the steep hill. Then she drew it in again on the downgrade, knowing it was more treacherous to be going down than up.

Some of her terror must have communicated itself to Mr. Holliday, she realized when he spoke again. "If I were as frightened of driving in snow and ice as you are, I would get an apartment in Carson City."

"I know it sounds silly, but I'm not afraid if I'm

11

the one behind the wheel," she told him.

"It doesn't sound silly at all. Everyone feels more confident when they're in control."

They reached another plateau and Leslie relaxed. They'd already gone past the outskirts of Virginia City and there was just one more hill to climb before they reached her Aunt Rose's house. Chances were good that Mitch LeBlanc had used his snowplow to clear the road. He and his invalid wife, Veronica, lived at the bottom of the hill, but Mitch obviously had his eye on Aunt Rose, so he went out of his way to do little things for her. Useless effort, because her aunt wouldn't look at a married man in the first place; and in the second place, she'd never shown the slightest inclination to change her widowed state during all of the six years since her husband died.

Sure enough, the road that led to the house was almost free of snow. "This is a welcome relief," Allan Holliday remarked as he pulled onto it.

"Our nearest neighbor lives at the foot of the hill and he's retired, so he has time to clear the roads and do other little kindnesses. I'm glad he's been out with his plow."

Leslie's mind was racing. Even though her aunt was not interested in a relationship with a member of the opposite sex, both Leslie and her mother felt she would be happier if she led a more active social life. At thirty-six, Rose Winters was a beautiful woman, but she seldom left the house on Silver Hill and the family was concerned that she would become an introverted recluse.

Allan Holliday was attractive, intelligent, and obviously kind. Otherwise, he wouldn't be driving her home in a snowstorm. He wasn't remotely like Mark Winters had been, which was an asset. A physical or

12

personality likeness to her husband would result in Rose making unfavorable comparisons. Because of the photographer's career, he would have a great deal in common with a woman writer, too, Leslie thought with growing excitement.

Just before they crested the hill, she said very casually, "My aunt will never forgive me if I don't insist that you come in. She'll be most grateful to you for bringing me home safely, and since I was already late when I left the office, she's probably been worried."

"What a beautiful house," Holliday said as he turned into the driveway. "A regular storybook place."

Lights shone from all the downstairs windows and the lamp on the columned front porch cast a golden glow on the white siding. The deeply drifted snow in the front yard added to the picturesque beauty of the scene.

"The original owner was Peter Overstock, a millionaire silver mogul," Leslie volunteered. "Aunt Rose inherited this house several years ago, at the same time my mother was bequeathed a Victorian beauty in San Francisco. We're distantly related to the Overstock family and it came as a lovely surprise when Mother and Aunt Rose were notified."

"Victorian right down to the leaded glass windows," Holliday said admiringly. He turned off the motor and added, "It looks inviting, like a place where people live and love. Please ask your aunt if I may have permission to photograph her house."

"I insist that you come in and ask her yourself," Leslie replied.

She had never assumed the role of matchmaker in

the past, but she didn't want to let the opportunity pass to introduce her aunt to Mr. Holliday. She liked him instinctively and was reasonably sure her aunt would find him attractive. On top of everything else, he looked as if he might be in the right age bracket, too. Somewhere around forty.

"She doesn't open the house to tourists, but I'm sure you'll find the inside even more beautiful than the outside."

"Thank you very much," he said. "But I don't want to intrude, and the snow is coming down faster and more furiously. I'd best get back to my hotel in Reno."

"*Reno!* Oh, they'll have closed off the highways to Reno long before now," she assured him.

Then she played her last card, knowing it was risky. Some men were merely bored at the notion of ghosts, while others were intrigued. For all she knew, Holliday was totally disinterested in hauntings, but the Overstock ghost was the only additional enticement she could offer.

"Maybe if you're lucky, the ghost will appear. It isn't often a photographer has a chance to take a picture of a person who's been dead for more than a hundred years."

II

For the past half hour Rose Winters had been anxiously looking out the front window hoping to see her niece's Volkswagen lights. If Mark were still alive he would have told her to stop worrying, then he would have poured a glass of sherry for her and insisted that she sit down on the sofa with him. He could always find a way to ease her mind. Her sister Irene often told her she must stop trying to bring her late husband back from the grave, but she took comfort in remembering the way Mark would do things. If only he hadn't died.

A car went by with the chains making loud squishy-clanking noises in the wet snow. Rose pressed her face against the window in order to see beyond her own reflection, taking courage in the realization that at least one automobile had made the steep grade. She thought she recognized the car as belonging to David Dedrick, who would be coming home from the university in Reno for the weekend. The Dedricks lived down the hill to her right, somewhat farther than Mitch and Veronica LeBlanc on the other side of her, but close enough to be considered neighbors. In the fall, after the leaves fell from the trees, she could see the lights in the windows of both houses from her own hilltop home.

With a forlorn sigh, Rose watched the winking red tail lights of the car that had just gone by until it turned into the Dedrick driveway. Her anxiety grew when she remembered that Leslie didn't have chains on her car. No use in telling herself to calm down, Leslie was quite able of taking care of herself. She, too, was capable of logical behavior when she was pressed, but she knew how treacherous it was to drive those snowy roads. She remembered Mark's referring to her capabilities. She could change a tire and put on chains. And she could make small repairs around the house, too. Once when Mark was away on a business trip she repaired the leaking roof on her San Francisco home because she couldn't find anyone else to do it and the ceiling was in danger of being ruined. Dealing with tasks that could be taken care of with tools was vastly different from dealing with her own emotions, though; and all sorts of terrible things could have happened to Leslie after she left Carson City. Her car could have stalled on any one of the hills. Or worse, gone off the road, plunging down hundreds of feet and there she would be, broken and bleeding.

"Oh, God," she said prayerfully. "Keep her safe from harm."

She loved her older sister's daughter as much as she would have loved a child of her own. She and Mark lived in San Francisco during all their years together and Leslie had spent as much time at their house as she did at home.

Futilely, she wished she hadn't sold the house where they'd lived all those years. When she first came to Virginia City she had lived in a tiny apartment while the workmen were restoring the old Overstock mansion she'd inherited. If she'd stayed in San Francisco, Leslie wouldn't be driving home in a snowstorm. Irene had argued against the move. She'd said Virginia City was too remote, an unlikely place for Rose to live alone, but she'd not been able to bear the San Francisco house where she kept looking for Mark in every room. The house had been a sanctuary for Leslie when she broke her engagement, and she did love the old place. Still, if she'd settled anywhere else, Leslie could have come there, and she simply hadn't thought about the impassable roads of winter when Leslie found employment in the State offices.

In the distance a set of headlights seemed to float through the darkness. Rose couldn't tell if they were close together like those of Leslie's car or far apart, which would mean they were on a larger vehicle. As the twin beams grew nearer, Rose grew more anxious. They didn't look like Volkswagen headlights. They grew brighter as the car rounded the treacherous curve at the bottom of the hill and she held her breath. Her spirits lifted when the car turned in at her lane. There. She'd been silly to let herself get all upset. Hurrying to the entry hall where she could get a better view, she looked outside and moaned in disappointment. The vehicle in her driveway was quite large and looked like a truck. Her heart pounded as she anticipated a stranger, someone to tell her Leslie had been in an accident.

She opened the front door and a gust of bitter cold wind blew her blue velvet hostess gown tightly

17

against her body. Snow stung her face and big feathery flakes nestled in her golden eyelashes. Two people ran up the place where the walk was buried under the snow, but the swirling flakes were so heavy she couldn't tell whether they were men or women. Leslie's lilting laughter sounded above the gusting wind and within a second Rose saw a tall man at her side.

"Oh, Aunt Rose, isn't this marvelous?" Leslie stamped her feet on the front porch and the man moved slightly to one side, his body language showing plainly that he didn't intend to stay. Leslie handed him a broom and told him to brush the snow from his boots. "I had car trouble, and this Good Samaritan drove me home."

Once inside, Leslie made the introductions. "Aunt Rose, may I present Mr. Allan Holliday? This is my aunt, Rose Winters. Remember, Aunt Rose, I told you he was doing a series on the State Capitols."

"Oh, yes, of course," Rose said. "Mr. Holliday, I'm so very grateful. I'll admit I was getting a bit worried about Leslie. Please come into the living room and we'll have a drink before dinner."

"Thank you, but I can't stay for dinner," Mr. Holliday responded. "I'll have a drink, then be on my way."

He took the chair Rose indicated, one that was near the warmth of the burning logs in the fireplace. Leslie asked him what he would like to drink and he said dry wine would be fine.

"I'll have sherry, dear," Rose said as she sank gratefully into a chair. She wasn't going to admit she'd been half out of her mind with worry, but now that Leslie was safely home her legs were too weak to hold her in a standing position.

She watched her niece as she moved about the room, aware of her beauty and grace. Leslie's long legs and stunning figure were a joy to behold. Rose had always been glad she had inherited the tall, lean build of the Ellisons instead of favoring the Delamar side of the family, all of whom were short in stature.

Mrs. Hanson came to stand in the doorway looking flustered. "You can't imagine how worried Mrs. Winters has been about you, Miss Leslie. And no *wonder!* According to the radio they've closed off Geiger Grade and there's a travelers' warning to stay off the roads. I just heard it on KOLO. There was a boy on a motorcycle that went off the road and got hisself killed, and I just don't know how many accidents they've been so far. They're saying this is about the worst blizzard in twenty years. I was wondering, Mrs. Winters, when you want dinner served."

"Give us fifteen minutes, Mrs. Hanson, and we'll have a guest," Rose said. The cook/housekeeper nodded and left, then Rose turned to Holliday with a smile.

"Whether you want to or not, Mr. Holliday, you'll have to spend the night."

"Oh, but I can take Gold Hill into Carson City," he said. "There shouldn't be a problem getting from Carson City to Reno."

"Good heavens," Rose exclaimed, "do you mean to tell me you've driven that road and didn't notice those dangerous curves? There are places where it could be certain death if you lost control. Since the highway department has closed Geiger Grade to traffic, that means Gold Hill is impassable. Even though you and Leslie were lucky enough to arrive safely, it would be sheer folly to try to go back the

19

way you came. There's a wind tunnel on the Hill road and sometimes an entire area is swept with what amounts to a small avalanche. It was almost five days before people could dig their cars out of the drifts on Gold Hill the last time we had a severe snow storm."

Holliday frowned. "That's long enough for people to starve to death if they didn't freeze first."

"They don't stay in the cars," Rose assured him. "They leave them and head home on foot. I take it you're not familiar with this part of the country, Mr. Holliday."

"No, I'm originally from North Carolina, but for the past several years I've lived in Florida." He looked around the room, his expression admiring. "This is a lovely home. One would almost expect to find furnishings like this in a museum. Shortly after I arrived in Carson City I was told a visit to Virginia City was in order, that the Chollar Mansion and The Castle were open to the public. Surely your home is every bit as elegant as the ones on the Historical tour, Mrs. Winters. Have you lived here long?"

"Five years," Rose answered. "We were living in San Francisco when my husband died. I came here two month after his funeral. This was orginally the Overstock Mansion. A few generations ago the Overstock brothers struck a rich silver vein. This house was Peter's and a duplicate of it was built for the other brother. It was about a hundred yards from this one, but it burned several years ago. The historical homes that are listed in the guide books to Virginia City aren't inhabited—there are only caretakers. I wouldn't dream of opening this place to the public."

"Surely it wasn't in this excellent condition when you moved in."

"Oh, no. It was deplorable. Several of the antiques were in good shape, though. The upholstery on almost all the Victorian furniture was in tatters. I think mice have a fancy for horsehair. But aside from the upholstery, the furnishings were easy enough to restore because the frames were intact. If you'd like, I'll show you through all the rooms."

"I'd enjoy it immensely. When I said the furnishings were museum quality I didn't mean your house looks as if no one lives in it. On the contrary, there's a feeling of contentment here. When we drove up, I told your niece the house looks like the kind of place where people live and love."

Rose wanted to tell him that yes, she lived, but her love was dead. Instead she said, "Mrs. Hanson will have dinner ready."

Leslie gave Mr. Holliday the directions to the downstairs bathroom where he said he would like to wash his hands. While he was out of the room, Rose took the opportunity to tell her niece her former fiance had called earlier in the day.

"You mean he came here to the house?" Leslie looked stricken.

"No, I mean he called on the telephone. He said he was in the vicinity and wanted to have lunch with you if it could be arranged. Since you told me not to let him know where you're working, I took the easy way out and lied. I said you hadn't found suitable employment as yet, and you'd gone to visit your mother. Probably I gave him the idea that you were thinking seriously about moving back to San

21

Francisco, too, but I didn't say so in actual words."

"It's just as well," Leslie said. "It would be very awkward to see Phillip right now." She smiled and put her arm around Rose. "Thanks for lying, Auntie. You're the limit."

Rose felt herself blushing again. It was against her principles to tell someone a bald-faced lie but she was well aware of her ability to do it convincingly, and Mark had always told her it was because she didn't do it often. She was concerned about the shadow that crossed Leslie's features at the mention of Phillip Tremont. Leslie had never confided her reason for breaking off with him, for actually calling off the wedding twenty-four hours before it was to take place, and Rose was not one to pry. All she really knew of the situation came from Irene when she called Rose to say there would be no wedding and Leslie was on her way to Virginia City. If Irene knew why Leslie waited until practically the last minute—with the bridal gown finished, all the bridesmaids arriving from distant states, the caterers in the process of preparing food for a hundred and fifty guests—she didn't say.

"You liked Phillip, didn't you?"

Leslie's question caught Rose by surprise. Two months before the wedding was scheduled, Leslie and Phillip came to spend a day with her. "He's very handsome," she said, choosing her words carefully, "and comes from a nice background. I found him intelligent and—well, yes, I did like Phillip."

She did not say that she'd noticed something lacking in the young man because she wasn't well acquainted with him enough to be absolutely positive that Phillip Tremont lacked a sense of humor. As far as Rose was concerned, anyone who married into the family would soon feel like an outsider if a sense of humor was lacking. They did a lot of laughing and talking when they got together and she'd been a trifle concerned about Phillip's air of brooding seriousness, a certain look about the mouth and in his eyes that seemed to say he was deeply worried about the state of the world or something of equal importance. On the other hand, she suspected that Leslie wished at times she hadn't changed her mind.

For the past few weeks Leslie had been dating David Dedrick, who resembled Phillip Tremont, and Rose had often wondered if Leslie was attracted to David because he looked like Phillip.

Mr. Holliday appeared in the doorway and they went in to dinner. Mrs. Hanson bustled around the table moving bowls an inch or two, looking worried. "Well, I don't know," she said. "I just don't know whether this meal will be fit to eat or not. A person can't hardly get good meat these days, and it didn't seem to me like the broccoli turned out just right. You know how I feel about those frozen vegetables, Mrs. Winters, but then a body has to make do with what's available and there's no fresh vegetables in that little dinky market uptown. I never did care much about February, even as a girl back home in Indiana I dreaded to see January end and February begin."

Allan Holliday added his assurance to the words of the others that the meal looked superb. The roast was done to a turn and the broccoli was reminiscent of a full page color advertisement in a woman's magazine the way it was nestled in a bed of creamy cheese sauce. Crispy brown braised potatoes were garnished with parsley and served in a ruby-red bowl. When Rose hired the Hansons as a couple,

Mrs. Hanson expressed her doubts about being able to please a "famous lady author." She said she was a plain country woman and did plain country-type cooking, yet she always presented meals which looked and tasted like holiday fare.

"I think I have everything on the table," she said with a doubtful look at the various serving bowls, "So me and Hanson will go ahead and sit down to eat. If you need anything, Mrs. Winters, just holler. One thing about it, though, I'm not a bit pleased with the way that apple pie turned out. It won't be fit to eat." With her words ringing in the air, the cook left the room.

"This is fare suitable for the gods," Allan Holliday said. "How strange of the cook to say she's not pleased with her efforts. I've never tasted such delicious beef before in my life."

"Mrs. Hanson is a chronic worrier," Leslie said.

"And she's over-imaginative, too," Rose added. "I'm lucky to have them, though. Mr. and Mrs. Hanson live in the caretaker's cottage behind the house."

She glanced around the room, pleased to be sharing a meal with a stranger. Overhead the crystal chandelier blazed with light. The cut glass drops tinkled musically now and then, sprightly accompanied to the howling wind outside. "That wind is ferocious," she said. "In spite of the storm windows, it's strong enough to move the draperies."

"And cause the chandelier baubles to tinkle," Leslie added. "You're shivering, Aunt Rose. I'll get a sweater for you." Rose thanked her.

Allan Holliday said, "I know you don't open your house to the public, but your furnishings are so beautiful and if you would allow me to take some photographs, it would be a way to share the beauty with others and not have hordes of people tramping through your home."

"All right," Rose said agreeably.

He asked her what kind of heating was installed and she said, "A coal furnace. Obsolete, but in fine working order. In time, I hope to utilize the hot springs for heating, but to date I've not been able to find anyone willing to do the work. The furnace was probably installed by one of the Overstock descendants who lived in the house after Peter died."

"Your niece informed me that your house came complete with a ghost," the photographer said. "Has anyone seen it?"

"I don't believe in ghosts and as far as I know, no one has seen it. According to local story teller, Peter Overstock never forgave his beautiful wife for letting him die in the icy waters of Lake Washoe. I've read the account of his death. It was taken from an eighteen-sixty-seven issue of *The Territorial Enterprise*. I can't see how she could have saved him since she couldn't swim. Neither could he, and that's why he drowned. Anyway, the old-timers insist that his voice has been heard by several people who've lived here, along with other ghostly goings-on. That's why it was unoccupied for many years."

"I've heard it," Leslie said as she entered the dining room with Rose's sweater.

"It's the wind," Rose stated with determination. "You know as well as I do the so-called phenomenon isn't audible unless there's a great deal of wind. Anyway, I've never been able to make out a single word."

Leslie smiled as she returned to the table. "It's

just that you don't want to admit there's a ghost lurking around, Aunt Rose." Turning to Holliday she said, "The voice is quite definite, and it's a man. He sounds angry and frightened and he says, 'Help, Beck!' Sometimes he's even more explicit. Then he says, 'Help me, Becky, damn you!' "

Holliday wanted to know more of the background and Rose supplied it: "Peter and Thurston Overstock came to Nevada from Georgia, hoping to strike it rich in silver. After a long struggle, they found a rich vein, and like most of the silver kings, the Overstock brothers wanted to display their wealth by building lavish homes with luxurious furnishings. They hired a local architect to draw plans, and both liked the same set of plans. So they built identical dwellings. Originally, Thurston courted a local school teacher, Becky Forsythe. But apparently Becky found Peter more to her liking since she married him and moved into this house as soon as it was finished. Meanwhile, Thurston corresponded with a young woman from back in Georgia, Martha Gillespie, and she came West to marry him. They moved into the other house, which was said to be identical to this one except for the heating plant. The hot springs I mentioned earlier lay directly under the Thurston Overstock house so they had steam heat while this place was originally equipped with a fireplace in each room. Since I own several acres, I intend to tap into the hot springs as soon as possible."

"Oh, but there's much more to the story," Leslie said.

Rose looked at her niece with a smile. "I didn't intend to drop it right there. All right, a year after Martha and Thurston were married, they had their first son. Within four years, they had three sons and a daughter. The last time Martha gave birth it was to twins. The Peter Overstocks remained childless and the old folk whose grandparents handed the story down insist that Peter blamed Becky because she didn't conceive, and he allegedly beat her severely, and often. There is one account in the court records that lends the legend some truth. Although women had no civil rights at that time, apparently Becky made a complaint against her husband through Thurston, who acted as her friend in court. He brought charges against Peter on Becky's behalf and I've read the transcripts. Peter was found guilty of mistreating his wife and was ordered to desist.''

"But she kept on living with him," Leslie said.

"Maybe she had no choice," Holliday pointed out. "There weren't any telephone numbers for battered wives to call when they needed help. Back in those days women had very little recourse."

"According to legend," Rose continued, "the brothers stopped speaking after Thurston publicly accused Peter of beating his wife. But Peter and Becky did continue living together and eventually Becky conceived. She was pregnant when Peter drowned in the icy depths of Washoe Lake. It happened on a Sunday afternoon after the Peter Overstocks visited with Sandy and Eilly Bowers. The Bowers' were also newly rich silver prospectors. Peter told Sandy Bowers he was going to take a short-cut home, he believed the lake was frozen solidly enough to withstand the weight of the carriage. Sandy was older and much wiser about the lake and advised Peter not to risk it. Becky allegedly begged her husband to head the horses on down the road, but he ignored her. She jumped out of the carriage at the last moment, but Peter drove on to the ice, screaming and swearing at her for disobeying him. She swore under oath that the ice gave away when he was just a few feet out and he plunged into the water over his head. Peter couldn't swim and neither could his wife, but according to her testimony at the Inquest, he expected her to save him. According to the testimony in the transcripts, Becky was afraid for him to try to drive over the ice, that she begged him to go the long way around. He laughed at her and called her a silly goose. When she jumped out, she said he swore at her and grabbed the horse whip, lashed at her with it but she escaped the blows. In his anger he dropped the whip to the ground, then sent the horses out on the ice.

"She turned back. It was her intention to walk on home. Then she heard the noise of the ice breaking and looked back in time to see the carriage going down, Peter screaming as he jumped to one side. Cracks formed in the ice at the place where the carriage went under and Peter slipped into the water. He grabbed at the edges of the broken ice and pulled himself back up until she could see his head and shoulders, she said. He shouted at her to come to him and bring the whip. She stated that she believed he intended for her to endanger herself and the child she was carrying by walking out on the broken ice floes in order to throw him one end of the buggy whip, then pull him to safety. Instead, she said she threw it toward him because the ice was breaking up all around him and she knew she would drown with him. He went down again and didn't come back up."

Allan Holliday looked pensive. "Think of the trauma the lady endured. Unless she was happy to see him drown and didn't try to save him. He had beaten her in the past and only moments before tried to hit her with the whip, when she jumped out of the carriage because she was afraid. A woman would naturally be concerned about the safety of her unborn baby, but still . . . I wonder if she simply turned her back on her husband?"

"According to the way the questions were put to her at the Inquest," Rose ventured, "it seemed to me the officials suspected she had. She stuck to her story, though, and the people who lived in a cabin near the lake testified that she was in a state of hysteria when she came for help. There was no trace of Peter Overstock, the horses, or the carriage, when the people went to see if they could help. It was two weeks before the authorities were able to get the body out of the water."

"What was the outcome of the Inquest?"

"I can't remember it verbatim, but the decision was that Peter Overstock met his death by accidental drowning. There was no trial."

"So the haunting of the house is due to Peter Overstock's sudden death," Holliday said.

"The *alleged* haunting of the house," Rose corrected him. "Don't tell me you believe Peter Overstock's restless spirit is still calling out to his wife after all these years."

Holliday laughed. "No, but I would believe it if I heard it. Especially if I had a chance to get a glimpse of him. What did the widow do after her husband died? Did she live out her life here in this house?"

"Oh, no, she rented the house to a miner's widow, then moved to San Francisco," Leslie supplied. "She built the place in San Francisco that my

29

mother inherited and lived the good life, but she never married again."

"Her baby was born prematurely and lived only a few days," Rose said. "Probably because of the accident, combined with the long walk to get help. According to the gossips, Thurston made regular trips to San Francisco after the tragedy and spent time with his widowed sister-in-law and he didn't take his wife along. Martha and Thurston had no more children, and the ones they had before Peter's untimely death all passed away when they were young. Martha died of the flu in 1917 and a year later Thurston was buried at her side. Becky outlived them all.

"My sister and I are descended from a younger brother of Peter and Thurston Overstock, and he inherited everything. His daughter married my grandfather, who was a Delamar. We had no idea of the relationship until my sister and I were contacted by the San Francisco bank after the last Overstock descendant died. They had been trying to find the rightful heirs for more than two years, and of course Irene and I were very happily surprised to learn—"

Rose stopped speaking when the lights went out.

III

Fighting panic, Leslie was barely aware of her
aunt's calm and reassuring words. "Just sit still,
Mr. Holliday. It doesn't happen often, but we're prepared for emergencies and the way the wind is
tearing things up out there it's no wonder the lights
went out."

"It isn't the wind, it's the ghost," Leslie said as
she left the table and felt her way to the rosewood
buffet where the candles were kept. Her fingertips
groped in the drawer and came into contact with the
smooth round tapers. She turned at a clicking
sound, ashamed of the way she'd jumped when she
realized it was Mr. Holliday's cigarette lighter. The
flame burned brightly and she went to it immediately, holding one of the candle wicks until it caught.

"I don't smoke, but a lighter often comes in
handy," he said.

Leslie's laughter sounded forced. She wished she
could get over the childish impulse to giggle nervously when she was afraid. Except for cutting

herself off in mid-sentence when the lights went off, her Aunt Rose was perfectly serene as she held three more candles to the flame of the first one, took the one Leslie was holding, and placed them all in the holders she had taken from the drawer. The sound of the kitchen door opening caused Leslie to jump again when Mrs. Hanson came in with a flashlight.

"If this don't beat all," the cook rasped. "Well, I see you've managed to get some light in the room." She stood uncertainly in the doorway, and Leslie was sure she intended to say something else.

"Everything is under control, Mrs. Hanson," Rose said with a smile. "I enjoy candle light. Lord knows it's flattering to faces that have lost the first blush of youth."

"Well, it's all right, I suppose," the cook said doubtfully, "but if it was left up to me, I'd rather light candles out of choice instead of necessity."

"We aren't ready for dessert just yet, Mrs. Hanson," Rose said rather pointedly. Leslie looked at her plate, realizing her aunt was being obvious, which was unusual. It was also out of character for Mrs. Hanson to stand in the doorway and say nothing.

"I know you're not ready for dessert, Mrs. Winters," the cook finally answered, "but I just— well, I'll tell you, Mrs. Winters, I don't like this being without electricity at all. That kitchen is as big as a barn. And besides—" The plump woman hesitated, her eyes large and luminous in the candle light, her right hand still gripping the flashlight. Behind her, the darkness loomed like a silent threat.

"You have candles in the kitchen, Mrs. Hanson, and your husband is with you," Rose said. Her voice was calm and reasonable.

"I know we've got candles in there, Mrs. Winters, but I'll just tell you this. We're the only house on the hill road that hasn't got any lights. I looked both ways and the Dedrick house is lit up just like the LeBlancs'."

Leslie shivered and instinctively looked toward the windows although she knew all the draperies were closed.

Allan Holliday stood up. "It's probably a fuse, then. Mrs. Winters, if you'll allow me, I'll check out the fuse box. If the wiring was installed years ago, there's a possibility of trouble from that direction. If the house was recently wired, it may be a circuit breaker."

Mrs. Hanson shifted her weight from one foot to the other and finally said, "Well . . . Hanson don't know anything about electricity and he's down in his back again real bad anyway. Every step he takes just about kills him."

Leslie understood the exasperated expression on her aunt's face. Rose was embarrassed, and preferred to react with anger. Quickly, she suggested that a line that led into the house might have blown down.

"Now, Miss Leslie," the cook said, "you know good and well there's no line down, and it's not any blown fuse, either. Or a circuit breaker that needs to be flipped back over. That only happens when there's an overload, and there wasn't a thing on in the house except the lights and maybe the refrigerator. And Mrs. Winters, there's no use in sitting there acting like everything's just hunky-dory, because I heard the ghost give the warning."

"What warning?" Leslie could tell by Holliday's voice that he was interested and alert.

Rose smiled, and Leslie heard a hint of ladylike sarcasm in her voice when the explained, "Mrs. Hanson is determined to keep the ridiculous ghost story alive."

Leslie's mother called Rose's tendency to ignore anything she didn't understand or disliked her one personality flaw. When her late husband's doctor took her aside and told her Mark Winters had but a short time to live, Rose refused to believe it. When he died, Rose refused to accept it. Once in a while Leslie felt called upon to act as a buffer between Rose's dream-world and reality, but not just then.

The cook put her hands on her hips. "You can act like I'm making it all up if you please, Mrs. Winters, but I tell you it's the truth. I heard the warning plain as day, calling just like it always does when it's getting ready to make itself known, and if turning out the lights on us isn't a sign that it's here, I don't know what is."

"It's the *wind*, Mrs. Hanson," Rose insisted.

"Hmph! Now who ever heard tell of a wind that can speak whole words? It says—"

"Mrs. Hanson, please." A more pronounced edge was in Rose's voice.

Mr. Holliday asked the cook to tell him what the voice said. He didn't know her aunt the way Leslie did.

"It says, 'Becky! Oh, Becky, damn you! Help me!'"

"Fantastic!" Holliday was enthusiastic. "First I'll check out the fuse box if you'll show me where it is, Mrs. Hanson, then I'd like to know more about this ghost of yours."

"It isn't my ghost," Mrs. Hanson retorted. "It lives here all the time and it has for years and years.

34

But you can only hear it at certain times." Warming to her subject, the older woman's voice filtered back to the dining room where Rose looked at Leslie and rolled her eyes.

"I can't fight you and Mrs. Hanson both," she said after a long pause. "And now, apparently Mr. Holliday is convinced there's an unearthly presence in the house. If that woman weren't such a great cook, I swear to goodness I would let her and her husband go." Rose Winters had often said that it was a good thing she didn't have to cook for a living.

Doors slammed and an icy blast raced through the dining room because the fuse box was in a utility room off the back porch. The candles flickered and Rose sighed. "I hope it *is* the circuit breaker," she said grimly. "It would teach you all a lesson."

Leslie ran her index finger across the patterned silverware. Although she had never mentioned her worries concerning her own mental stability, there were times when she wondered if she was sane. Calling off a wedding the day before it was to take place wasn't a sign of rational behavior, people would likely say. Everyone in the family supposed the break came about over a difference of opinion which had turned into a full-fledged quarrel, but that wasn't the case. She hadn't told anyone why she did it because she was too upset about the whole thing, and she'd maintained silence about the subject for three months because she just didn't want to think about it. She should have told her mother, at least, what it was all about, and now that months had passed she felt acute embarrassment at disclosing the disgusting details.

Then there were the roses. When she first met Phillip he sent her roses frequently, and she had loved them. Red roses, with long stems, and she had planned to carry them in her bridal bouquet. Yes, she adored roses—but she had never expected to see them blooming outside in midwinter. Of course not. Yet she had seen them on the day of the first snow of the season. She had just happened to look out her bedroom window after she awakened and there were roses outside, blooming in the snow.

Winter roses, she had thought as she raced downstairs in her nightgown. Fortunately, she had awakened early that morning, and her aunt was still in her bedroom. Otherwise, Leslie would have said something foolish to her about the roses in the snow. When she opened the front door she saw nothing but white and glittering snow. She was positive that she had imagined the roses, so she said nothing about them. But it was reasonable to believe that if she could conjure up a dozen or so beautiful blooms, she could also convince herself the house was inhabited by a ghost.

The back door opened again, sending another gust of freezing air into the house. Allan Holliday came back to the dining room looking cold. "No circuits are broken, and I couldn't see any lines down. Of course it's difficult to see in the dark, even with a flashlight, and it's still snowing hard."

Mrs. Hanson was right behind him. "It's just like the last time, remember, Mrs. Winters? We had the living room all torn up because of the painters that were doing the woodwork and the lights went out, but only *here*, on the top of the hill! That was just before Miss Leslie came. Then, right before the lights came on, we heard the voice calling out for Becky to come and help him."

"*You* heard it, Mrs. Hanson," Rose said firmly. "*I* didn't."

"The lights are on in the Hanson's cottage," Holliday said. "And I could see lights in the windows in both houses down the hill."

"I suggest that you and Mr. Hanson go on home for the evening, Mrs. Hanson," Rose said. "We'll manage quite nicely, in spite of no electricity."

"The mister has gone down to bank the furnace for the night, ma'am. He held the flashlight while the gentleman looked at that box. Like I told you when we first came to work, Hanson isn't no hand with electricity." The cook wrung her hands and seemed to be listening for something. "You're sure you'll be all right, now, Mrs. Winters? I'll just tell you the truth, I feel downright creepy in this great big house without lights and all."

"All I'm worried about is a fire," Rose answered. "Obviously, there's a short in the line, otherwise we wouldn't have this trouble. Which upsets me greatly since the electricians who re-wired the place for me were highly recommended."

Without warning, the lights came back on and as soon as her eyes had adjusted to the sudden brightness, Leslie looked at her aunt and saw a flash of triumph in her eyes. She wasn't surprised when Rose said, "*There!* And without a voice from the grave saying we would now have light!" She turned to the others, and demanded, "Or did everyone else hear it? Am I ignoring the existence of a supernormal intelligence because I'm too stubborn to hear it?"

"No, Aunt Rose," Leslie answered. "No voice." She was intensely relieved.

Mrs. Hanson served a beautiful apple pie, her usual good nature restored now that the lights were back on. Rose suggested they have coffee in the living room and after everyone was served Mrs. Hanson said she would tidy up the kitchen and go home. The logs in the fireplace had burned low and Holliday replenished them. He offered to take a look at the wiring the next morning since Rose had mentioned a possible fire hazard. Politely, she said it could wait until the roads were passable and she would call an electrician.

"No, I insist," the photographer said. "A loose connection or damaged insulation can pose a very real threat, and I'm no stranger to electrical circuits. My father ws a contractor before he retired, and I did the wiring to help defray my college expenses." He looked at the grand piano in the corner. "Do you play, Mrs. Winters?"

"No, my husband was a musician. Just as you helped put yourself through school doing electrical work, he played the piano in night clubs in order to get through law school."

Leslie jumped to her feet when her aunt mentioned law school. She had forgotten her date with David Dedrick, who was in his final year of pre-law at the University of Nevada. "David and I planned to go down to the Yellow Dog tonight," she said. "But that was before the storm. I wonder if he was able to get home. I'll go call his house and see." As she was leaving the room she heard Mr. Holliday asking what on earth The Yellow Dog was and her aunt's reply that it was a saloon, of sorts, the only one in town that stayed open through the winter months.

When she lifted the telephone from the cradle she

38

didn't hear a dial tone, but the service was undependable during the winter at best, so she thought nothing of it. Just as she was leaving the family room, she heard the tinkle of sleigh bells and smiled. David had mentioned a sleigh, but she hadn't dreamed he would brave the storm just to keep a date. She opened the door in time to see him leap down into the snow, then run toward the house in his usual style. "I've been trying to call you, Dave," she called to him.

"The phones are out all over town," he said as he brushed the snow from his boots. "Brrr! It's colder than blue billy hell, whatever that means, but Sugar was raring to go. She loves the sleigh. Whose four-wheeler?" He inclined his dark head toward the driveway and she explained about having car trouble and told him Allan Holliday had brought her home.

After she closed the door she whispered, "I think Aunt Rose is rather taken with him. She's agreed to let him photograph the inside of the house."

David was always assured of a welcome at the Winters' house. His mother and father came to call on Rose the day she moved in and brought along a casserole, which they said was a traditional welcome to a new neighbor. They respected her need for privacy and never dropped in without an invitation, and they were the only residents of Virginia City who had dined at her home. Leslie knew Rose approved of David because he was going to law school, didn't wear his hair too long and played the piano. She had made it clear that she felt David would be an exceptionally fine husband if Leslie would only give him some serious thought, but Leslie was not ready to make another commitment.

Early in their friendship she told David she felt her aunt lived too quietly, that she had all but stopped living after her husband died. Rose Winters continued to write her best-selling murder mysteries, but the nature of her career aided her tendency to withdraw from life. Leslie felt that thirty-six was too young to live on memories and David agreed with her. One of the reasons she had come to Virginia City after she cancelled her wedding was because of her concern about Rose. She had hoped to coax her reclusive aunt into leading a more social life, but until Allan Holliday happened along when she needed him, she had met no one she felt Rose would be comfortable with.

Rose greeted David with a glowing smile. After she introduced him to Allan Holliday she said, "But you don't plan to go to town in this dreadful storm, do you?"

"Oh, no, they've closed down the Yellow Dog and there's not a car on the road," David assured her. "But I couldn't get a dial tone and then found out all the phones were out and Sugar was champing at the bit, wanting to take me for a sleigh ride. Besides, I wanted to make sure Leslie arrived safely."

Holliday mentioned the few minutes when they'd been without electricity. David said they'd had no power outage at their house, perhaps they were on a different line. Then he looked at Rose and grinned. "Are you sure it wasn't old Peter the Terrible showing off, Rose?"

"Not really," she answered with an easy laugh. David was the only person Leslie knew who could joke with her aunt about the well-known Overstock ghost. "I'm sure Leslie is positive the ghost had something to do with the power outage, and Mrs.

Hanson is absolutely unreasonable. She insists she heard the eerie voice just before the lights went out, but no one else did. Mr. Holliday probably thinks he's landed in a house full of demented creatures."

The photographer shook his head. "No, but I'm quite interested in the supernatural. It would please me greatly to photograph a spirit, but I have an idea Mrs. Winters was on the right track when she said a shorted-out wire was responsible for the temporary outages."

Rose asked David if he would play for them, but he said he didn't want to keep the horse out in the weather any longer than neceessary. "Another time, though. Maybe tomorrow night, because the snow is still coming down so we'll have to stay at home and entertain ourselves."

Leslie walked him to the front door and when they were out of hearing distance of the living room, he made a circle with his index finger and thumb, then winked. "You're absolutely right. Rose is fairly sparkling. How long is Mr. Holliday going to be in Carson City?"

"Another week, I think, but I'm not really sure."

"Great. By then, maybe they'll have progressed beyond the Mr. Holliday and Mrs. Winters formality. Look, if you're worried about your Volkswagen, I can probably get down the hill tomorrow in the sleigh. I doubt if there'll be a garage open with a mechanic on duty, but I'll take a look at it, maybe get it inside someone's garage."

"Oh, no, David, it'll be all right. By Monday morning, the roads will be clear and the service stations will be open. The car is perfectly all right where it is."

He told her he would see her the following

evening, even if he had to come by snow shoe, and left. For a second, Leslie felt a wave of emptiness, which she recognized after deep thought as disappointment because David hadn't kissed her. He never had, but she had been careful to let him know without putting it into words that she didn't want to be kissed. On the other hand, maybe he hadn't wanted to in the first place.

As she went back to the living room she thought of a word her mother had recently used to describe Rose: *Peculiar*. Rose had always been reserved, she remembered her mother saying, but after she met and married Mark Winters she blossomed into a vivacious, exciting woman. Leslie hoped David didn't consider them both as peculiar. On the surface she was bubbling and effervescent. She consciously tried to overcome her natural shyness and most of the time she felt she succeeded. But it miffed her a little to realize she had wanted David to take her in his arms and kiss her, miffed her more because he hadn't. David was intelligent and possessed tremendous insight. She was suddenly unsure of herself and inwardly winced at the idea that he found her unattractive. Strange.

He knew about the wedding that didn't happen because she told him, and part of her turmoil concerned the statement Rose had recently made to her about the physical resemblance between David and Phillip. Leslie disagreed. They both had dark hair and blue eyes, but their features were not in the least similar. And as far as personalities were concerned, they were at extreme ends of the pole. No, she wasn't setting herself up for another broken romance, she told herself severely. And she wasn't peculiar, either.

"If it's all right with you, I think I'll go to bed," she said to her aunt when she was back in the living room. Then she almost laughed out loud at the look of consternation that crossed Rose's face. Clearly, her aunt was telling her she didn't want to be left alone with a man. Allan Holliday either understood how his hostess felt or he was genuinely tired. He said he would like to turn in, too, that the day had been a long one for him.

The second floor was divided by a carpeted stairway and a long hall. Originally, there had been six bedrooms upstairs, but there had been no bathrooms or clothes closets. A lavish bathroom had been installed on the west side which utilized the middle bedroom. The fixtures were turn-of-the-century in style. The tub was enormous, had ball feet with eagle claws, and someonee with tastes much different from hers had painted the outside of the tub a violent shade or purple. Rose had had the bathtub scraped to the raw metal, then painted with gleaming white epoxy, but she'd not been able to resist the temptation presented by the ball and claw feet. The balls were gold leaf, the claws realistically bird-foot color, which Leslie disliked. Nor did she care for the pink marble walls, the pedestal washbowl surrounded by more of the pink marble, the ornate toilet that looked more like a throne than a bathroom fixture, yet Rose luxuriated in the huge bathroom, right down to the furry white carpet on the floor and all those little extras. Rose liked the gold toothbrush holder and matching soap dishes with a golden water nymph for a pedestal for each one. Matching gold towel bars, even the cover for the light switch, was in the shape of a water nymph.

The third bedroom on the west side had been converted into a dressing room and walk-in closet which held a shocking number of Rose Winters' clothes. Leslie was amazed when she counted twenty at-home gowns until she remembered that her aunt seldom left the house. The closet held at least a hundred pairs of shoes, most of them impossibly out-dated, but Rose liked to see them there and took her niece's teasing in stride. "You're getting older too, Leslie," she said in one of her rare impish moods, "but you'll always be my favorite niece, and I'll never send you to the Salvation Army or the Good Will just because you're obsolete."

Leslie liked the east side of the upstairs much better. The bedroom at the far end was used for storage. The guest bedroom and the one at the foot that Leslie claimed were separated by a compact but efficient bathroom with a no-nonsense look. Rose turned down their guest's bed while Leslie explained about the shared bathroom.

"We keep the doors closed all the time, but we lock them only when we're using the john," she said. "Just don't forget to unlock my side when you leave, otherwise, I'll have to disturb Aunt Rose or come barging through your room. The alternative is to go downstairs, and I'm a little uneasy about going down there with a ghost on the loose, maybe the lights going off."

"Dear heavens, Leslie," Rose said after she finished fussing with the pillows on the guestroom bed, "you're nineteen years old. Far too old to be afraid of the dark. Anyway, Mr. Holliday is going to check out the wiring tomorrow, so you won't have to be afraid of being caught downstairs in the dark." She turned at the doorway and said goodnight.

Leslie heard her small feet pattering across the hall and smiled at Allan Holliday.

"She is without a doubt the most fascinating woman I've ever met," he told her. "And so utterly beautiful, too. I—" He looked at her and put his hand over his mouth. "I'm sorry I spoke so impulsively. It's one of my most glaring faults."

Leslie smiled. Speaking softly, she said, "She's very lonely, but she doesn't realize it. Aunt Rose finds it easy to ignore things that don't suit her. Her late husband was convinced that it was a charming trait, but he was delighted with everything about her. Good night, Mr. Holliday, and thanks again for rescuing me."

Five minutes later, Leslie stepped out of the shower, dried herself and slipped her nightgown over her towel-wrapped head. She used a blow drier on her long hair in the bedroom and quickly got in bed, brushed her hair and opened the book she'd been reading the night before. After the third chapter, the print began to blur and she turned out the light on the night table, settled herself more comfortably against her pillow and went to sleep.

Her own voice awakened her from slumber. She had laughed in her sleep. Wishing she hadn't disturbed the pleasant dream she'd been enjoying, she turned over and listened to the barely audible sound of the snow blowing against the window, the quiet serenity of the house. She was warm, comfortable and relaxed. It was unusual for her to awaken during the night, but the few times she had since she'd moved in with her aunt she'd been slightly uneasy, too aware of living in a secluded house where the dead were said to roam.

Knowing Allan Holliday was in the room that adjoined her bathroom made a world of difference. She hoped her attempts at matchmaking would work. She snuggled down deeper under the blankets and was about to drift off again when the voice— if it was a voice—came plaintively from everywhere and nowhere, all at once.

"Becky! Come to me, Becky, ohhhhhhh—help me. Help me!"

If she had been jolted by several volts of electricity, Leslie would have reacted the same way. She convulsed, then went rigid, all in a space of what couldn't have been more than a tenth of a second.

IV

Rose prepared for bed as usual. A creature of habit, she followed the same routine that had suited her for years. Once she turned out the light, turned over and arranged her pillow the way she always did, she turned her thoughts to her current book. When she first began writing, she fell into the habit of planning the next chapter just before she went to sleep. If something came along that interferred with her schedule of working out dialogue and strategy, her writing didn't flow as well the following day. That night she found it difficult to concentrate. She pictured her fictitious characters and put them into their various roles, gave them words to say as always, but Allan Holliday's face kept inserting itself into her story, and her mind wandered.

Instead of mentally planning the next day's work, she recalled the pleasant timbre of his voice, the way she had felt when she told him goodnight. Like a blushing schoolgirl, she realized, in shame. It was embarrassing to find herself attracted to him when she'd never intended to let herself love again. No, absolutely not, she wasn't going to get involved. Mark was a wonderful husband, she reminded herself. They'd had a fine marriage. But Mark left her. It had not been his intention to die and leave her; she was sensible enough to know he hadn't wanted to die, but the results were the same as if he'd left her for another woman and she wasn't going to risk being plunged into the depths of despair again. Besides, she was foolish to even think Allan Holliday was attracted to her. Good heavens, she told herself severely, the man was cordial, but nothing more.

Once again, she brought back her fictitious characters and picked up the thread of her story, pushed away the stray thoughts that slipped into her mind and knew precisely how she would write the next day's chapter before she went to sleep. She had reached the point of total oblivion when the voice awakened her.

Her first reaction was to hold her breath and listen. She wanted to put her hands over her ears and close out the dreaful whimpering, sighing words that drifted into her dark bedroom. The flesh of her arms broke out in cold chills when the words came again, clear, yet muted. She drew in a deep breath and screamed.

Holliday's voice sounded immediately afterward. "Good God!" The two words sounded harsh and explosive to Rose as she sat up in bed, then fumbled with shaking fingers for the light. She put her feet into her slippers and grabbed her dressing gown before she left the room.

Leslie stood in the hall, just outside her bedroom door, her face as white as paper. Holliday burst through the door of his bedroom and looked around.

"It was just the wind," Rose insisted, calm now after her sudden fright. "Why, I know of a house in California where the wind plays an actual melody when it blows a certain way. Because of the way the gutters and downspouts were constructed, probably."

"But these were words, Aunt Rose," Leslie cried. "Real *words!*"

Rose looked at her guest. Before then it hadn't occurred to her that he wouldn't have pajamas. He wore nothing but a pair of pants and a strange expression. "It wasn't the wind," he stated. "It was definitely a voice, and the words were distinct." Crossing the hall quickly, he spoke to Rose in a near-whisper. "I think you're the victim of some sort of a cruel hoax."

"Maybe we'd better go downstairs," Rose said. "I doubt if anyone will be able to sleep for a while after this . . . whatever it was." No matter what happened she wasn't going to stand around in the hall with a partially dressed man.

"I'm afraid to go back to my bedroom for a housecoat," Leslie said.

"I'll go with you," Rose answered as she crossed the hall decisively. She waited while Leslie shrugged into a woolly robe and put on bedroom slippers, paying very little attention to her prattle about hearing actual words, they were clear as day and obviously spoken by Peter Overstock's ghost.

"You're hysterical," Rose said as they left the bedroom. "Try to calm down. There's a perfectly normal explanation for what we heard. Didn't Irene ever tell you about the house in Ohio where we lived during our childhood? There were all kinds of strange noises in that house, but the most annoying sounded like a flute. Our father found the cause and fixed it. It was nothing but a piece of weatherstripping that had worked loose around the back door. Of course your mother and I were terrified of the house, even after Dad found the source and stopped it."

"Aunt Rose," Leslie said as they went downstairs, "you're not fooling me. You're grasping at straws! You looked like a ghost yourself when you came out of your bedroom. Your hair was practically standing on end."

"I was—ah—momentarily frightened, I'll admit— but then I came to my senses and realized there was no one skulking about in my bedroom. Now—" Rose cleared her throat and appeared to have at least convinced herself that nothing was really wrong. "We'll make some hot chocolate."

She hoped Mr. Holliday as well as Leslie would go out to the kitchen with her so she wouldn't be alone. Just in case neither one of them volunteered, she said, "Let's all go out to the kitchen, sit down and talk about this—whatever it was—in a calm and dignified way."

Allan Holliday put on his shirt and slipped into his shoes before he came down. While Rose made hot chocolate, he sat at the table with Leslie. "I'm serious about the possibility of someone trying to frighten you out of this house, Mrs. Winters. Has anyone offered to buy it?"

"No. At least not lately," Rose said as she stirred the milk into the chocolate and sugar.

"Would you sell if someone asked to buy? If you were offered a good price?"

"I don't know. But I don't think so."

"Maybe there's a silver mine under the house or somewhere on the property," Leslie suggested.

"Not a chance," Rose answered. "There is a tunnel that leads from this house to the place where Thurston and his wife lived. Most of Virginia City is built above mines, as far as that goes. But it isn't profitable to work the silver, what little is left."

"And there's a basement," Holliday mused while Rose put the cups of steaming hot chocolate on the table. "I'm not an overly imaginative person, yet I heard several words being spoken. I wasn't asleep, so I couldn't have been dreaming." He looked directly at Rose. "In order for a voice to be heard all over the house, it would have to come from a central location with outlets in every room. I'm guessing the source is the furnace, and I'd like to go down and take a look at it."

"There's a fire in the furnace," Rose said. "How could anyone climb inside and call for help, projecting a voice through the heating ducts?"

Leslie giggled. "So you did hear it after all."

"All right," Rose said wearily. "I heard it and it scared me half to death."

"It wouldn't be necessary to climb inside a furnace in order to send a voice through the heating ducts," Holliday said. "There's a draft regulator on the back of most coal furnaces that would serve as an amplifier. Who offered to buy the house, Mrs. Winters?"

"Doctor Kellerman. He lives in town and shortly after I began to have the work done on the place he came to the hotel where I was living and made a reasonable offer."

"A medical doctor, single and captivated by Aunt Rose," Leslie said. She got up and went to the

51

window where she cupped her hands around her eyes to look out. "It's still snowing, and there are places where it's drifted at least four feet high. Doctor Kellerman is far too sensible to come out in a snowstorm to play a trick." Automatically she looked at her watch, which she usually left on her wrist at night even though she'd been told it was not good for the works. "It's after one o'clock in the morning. No one would—" Her hand went to her heart and she stared at Holliday, frightened. "What if someone's still down there?" Without thinking, she ran across the room to make sure the bolt was shot on the door that led to the basement. She turned, terrified at the idea of someone lurking in the shadows, ready to pounce in case someone came down to investigate. "I'd rather believe it's Peter Overstock's spirit," she said in a shaky voice.

No sound from outside gave a warning that anyone was close to the house and all three of them jumped nervously when a knock sounded at the door. Rose stared at the door, her eyes wide. "Who can that be at this time of the night?" She felt weak and knew the color had drained from her face.

The knock came again and from outside someone called, "Oh, Rose, are you in there?"

"Oh, Lord," Rose said in dismay. "That's Mitch LeBlanc."

"Our neighbor to the left," Leslie explained, "the one who clears the snow from the road."

Rose opened the door and gave Mitch a cold smile. "Come in," she said because she was too well bred to say anything else. "What brings you out in this storm, Mitch?"

Mitch stamped the snow from his boots. "Veronica wasn't able to sleep and I was in the kitchen when I saw a light up here, Rose. So I thought maybe someone was sick and came on up the hill." All the time he was speaking he cast covert glances at Allan Holliday. "Saw a strange vehicle in your driveway, too."

"Nothing's wrong. We were late getting to bed, Mitch," Rose said, unwilling to mention the real reason they were in the kitchen at one o'clock in the morning. She introduced the two men and offered LeBlanc a cup of hot chocolate, but he declined. Rose explained about Leslie's car trouble and that Mr. Holliday was kind enough to bring her home from work. Then she said, "Mitch has been very kind to me since I moved in. He found reliable carpenters, plumbers and electricians, told me the best places to buy material—Mitch, maybe you'd like a bit of brandy."

"Don't mind if I do," LeBlanc said as he took a chair. He was a big, blustering man with a shock of greying red hair that blew in the wind during the warm months and was kept tucked under a red and black hunting cap when it was cold. In spite of his untiring efforts to please her, Rose found him distasteful. His voice was a shade too loud, his friendliness too obvious. She was often irritated by his statements to the effect that she was a little widow-woman, all alone and without a man to protect her, but more than anything else she resented his thinly veiled attempts to become more than neighborly. He gave Leslie a look of disappointment and spoke almost paternally. "You should of called *me*, honey. I would of been tickled to death to come into Carson and get you."

"Mr. Holliday just happened to be there," Leslie said with a smile. "So it worked out for me very nicely. He's doing a picture story on State Capitols." She wondered why their guest left the table and went to stand at the window where he peered out into the night.

Mitch put his big hands around the brandy glass Rose gave him and nodded. "A photographer, huh? Well, my line was more strenuous. I ran a bulldozer for a construction outfit in Reno before I got into real estate. Say, Rose, another reason I thought I'd better get up here and see if you little ladies needed any help was on account of I thought I seen Doctor Kellerman's sleigh goin' by the house about a half-hour ago. Could of been mistaken, but I figgered he'd been here."

"No, he wasn't here, Mitch," Rose said with a forced smile.

"A real smart man, Doctor Kellerman," Mitch continued after he slugged down the brandy. "At least that's what they say. I never got through high school myself, but I made a good livin'. Not as good as a doctor, but I done all right." His booming laugh bounced around the room. "I guess Kellerman is kind of sweet on Rose, but she sent him packin' right off the bat." His eyes fell on Rose in a proprietary manner and she felt the flesh at the back of her neck crawl. Not only was he casting a proprietary look at her, his attitude conveyed protectiveness and a certain amount of good humored denial that Rose could not possibly be interested in Doctor Kellerman or anyone else as long as *he* was on the scene.

To her surprise, Allan Holliday gave Mitch a cold look and said, "Perhaps you were mistaken."

Mitch jerked his head around and blustered. "No way. The Doc came right out and told me Rose turned him down flat. Myself, I thought he was kind of rushin' things a bit, you know. But that's how men are when they've got a string of fancy degrees. I could of told him how the little lady stood." He got to his feet and patted Rose's shoulder.

"I turned Doctor Kellerman down when he asked to buy my house," Rose said. "I can't understand how you got the impression that it was a proposal."

Mitch grinned. "Well, I'll be dad-burned. I guess that's the way gossip gets started, you know? Hell, I'd a swore he meant marriage. What did he want with this place, anyway?"

Relieved that he was heading toward the door, Rose kept a civilized smile in place. "I suppose he likes the house, Mitch. So nice of you to be concerned and please give Veronica my best regards." She spoke the last few words as she opened the door for him, refrained from slamming it after he left and turned back to Leslie and Allan Holliday. "Honestly that *man!*" She sat down at the table and tasted her hot chocolate, found it had grown cool and pushed it away.

Allan Holliday asked, "How much did Kellerman offer?"

Rose was startled. "Why, uh, seventy-five thousand dollars," she said after a slight pause. "That was before all the restoration was completed."

Holliday nodded, went over to the counter where he picked up a flashlight. "Is it all right if I take a look at the basement?"

Rose shot a quick look at Leslie. "We'll all go. But you won't need a flashlight, there are plenty of electric lights down there."

"The power could go off," Holliday said. "It has

before, and I'd rather be ready."

Basements had never been Rose's favorite places, but she wasn't going to let him go down alone. "I'll go with you."

Leslie shrieked, "I'm not going to stay in this kitchen by myself."

The three of them went down the stairs after Rose turned on the light. A narrow hall was at the end of the flight, and Rose reached inside the wall to her left to turn on the overhead lights in the entire basement area. The room that was to the left of the hall was obviously used for a laundry. A gleaming washer and dryer along the front wall contrasted sharply with an obsolete laundry tub and a small, ancient, wood-burning stove. Rose explained that she'd left the little laundry stove where it was because someone had told her it was a collector's item. "This is the only basement room that didn't have a dirt floor when I moved in," she said, "but the concrete was beginning to crumble so as long as I had to have new floors poured in the rest of the rooms, I had this one done over." Except for the clothes chute, which Rose had recently had installed so Mrs. Hanson wouldn't have to carry the laundry downstairs, nothing else was in the small basement room to the left.

"That's a curious door," Holliday said, nodding toward the end wall of the laundry room where a rested iron door was set into the masonry. "Does it lead to a fruit cellar?"

"No, the fruit cellar is across the hall," Rose said. "That door was apparently installed by Peter Overstock and it opens into a tunnel that connects with the ruins of the Thurston Overstock house. I've never wanted to explore the tunnel so I didn't bother to have the padlock removed. I'm sure the tunnel is inhabited by all sorts of creepy, crawling things like rats and snakes, spiders and other creatures I don't even like to think about. There's an identical door in the remains of the Thurston Overstock basement, and it's padlocked from the inside of what's left of the basement, too. At least it was when I was there a month ago."

Holliday stepped across the room to inspect the door. He looked at the rusted padlock, made sure it was locked and touched the bolt. "The bolt looks strong enough to keep the creatures safely confined inside the tunnel, but with the padlock in place, there's no reason to suspect anyone of getting inside the house through the tunnel."

They went back to the hall and Rose pointed out the wine cellar in the space opposite the laundry room and the shelves that had been built for storing canned goods. On the far wall was a small cellar, actually more rightly called a dug-out area, that provided a place where root vegetables and fruits could be wintered over. There was no exit from it, and the air was dank and stale.

"That's all there is," Rose said, "except for the furnace room. Because of the automatic fireman, it requires considerable space."

The three of them filed into the big room where a monstrous furnace with a huge automatic fireman along one side of it dominated one wall. The photographer went to the back of the furnace and beamed the flashlight on the draft control. It was closed, so he opened it by hand and held it while he called into the metal ductwork. "Hall-ooooooo!" His voice sounded hollow and slightly muffled. "If you'll go back upstairs and listen," he suggested, "I'll stay

57

down here and wait until I hear footsteps overhead, then I'll call into the hole again."

Reluctantly, the two women went upstairs and stood in the middle of the living room floor. Seconds later Holliday's voice floated into the room. "Rose Winters," he called. Then, "Leslie Ellison." Rose and Leslie looked at one another. Even though she knew Holliday was downstairs in the basement creating the sound on purpose, Rose broke out in cold chills. There was a disembodied quality to the voice. An other-worldness that smacked of all the tales of horror she had read as a young girl. "That's it," she said to Leslie when she was able to speak in a normal tone. "Not the same voice, but the same general kind of eerie, floating sound. If I didn't know it was being directed into the ductwork, I wouldn't realize the main force of it came from the floor registers."

"Because it's all over the house at once," Leslie said. "Coming from every room at the same time, but not from anyplace in particular."

Holliday ran up the steps, through the kitchen and dining room and confronted them in the living room. "How did the sound compare with the one we heard earlier?"

Rose and Leslie spoke together. "Almost identical."

Rose drew her robe closer and shivered. "Which means you were right when you said you supected someone of playing a cruel hoax." She blinked, wanted to tell him he was exceptionally clever to have figured out the source of the voice in such a short time, but she was unable to put her thoughts into words.

"I'm not sure I'm right about my theory, but

we've found what may be the source. The thing is, there's a lot of snow on the ground. If someone stood behind the furnace long enough to send an excellent imitation of a ghostly message through the heating ducts, why are there no traces of melted snow in the basement? I checked every square inch of floor as well as the steps, but I saw no drop of melted snow, no suspicious looking tracks of any kind. The concrete floor is bone dry."

"Overshoes," Rose said. "What if the person wore overshoes, took them off before going to the basement, maybe wore nothing under them but stockings."

"There would be tell-tale tracks in the snow. When Mr. LeBlanc was here, I went to the window and looked out. His footsteps were very clear where he waded through the snow. I could see them as far away as the road in front of the house. It's still snowing, but the wind is no longer blowing, so any tracks that were made within the past few hours should still be visible. I'll go out and check around. The basement windows are firmly locked, so entrance had to be made by the front or back door. Unless someone came in through one of the downstairs windows."

"No, they're all locked from the inside," Rose said.

"Better check to make sure," Holliday insisted as he went to the hall closet for his coat. "But I wouldn't be surprised to find a set of footprints outside one of the doors." He went out the front door and Rose ran to turn on the porch light. She looked out in time to see him bound down the steps, then stand very still while he shone the flashlight around the front yard. The drifts that had formed before

Leslie and Holliday arrived had grown deeper, but there were no dark indentations that she could see except for a double set of tracks where Mitch LeBlanc had come to the house, then left.

Leslie was methodically going from window to window to make sure the locks were secure and Rose went to the back door to turn on the outside light. Holliday trudged through the deep snow with effort. Some of the drifts were above his knees, Rose noted. She watched while he sent the circle of light from the flashlight back and forth across the vast whiteness in the back yard, then shone it toward the rear of the house until the cottage where the Hansons lived was briefly outlined in a pale orange glow. She opened the door and called out. "Nothing?"

He shook his head. "Not a track, except for the ones made by LeBlanc."

"Come in before you freeze," she said, trying to ignore the little spark of pleasure she took from having someone to fuss over. Leslie had never liked to be hovered over, not even when she was a little girl. Mark enjoyed the personal attention she lavished on him, the special dishes she prepared for him, her concern for his well-being. For the first time since her husband died she realized she liked having a man of her own to "do" for and it was pure instinct that caused her to brush the newly fallen snow from the shoulders of his coat, then hand him a towel so he could dry his hair. Her cheeks turned pink when he thanked her. Mark often told her how much he appreciated her thoughtfulness. But he was equally considerate, which was one of the many reasons why their marriage was so wonderful. Her eyes filled with tears because of the empty ache in her heart, but she carefully averted her face to keep Allan Holliday from seeing them.

In a voice as casual as she could muster, she said, "Since the snow hasn't been disturbed, it looks as if we're back to Square One. How could someone get in the basement, call through the heating ducts, but not disturb the snow?"

Leslie came into the kitchen and said all the windows were locked. She looked at Holliday questioningly. "No footprints?"

"None," Holliday answered. "Except the ones left by Mitch LeBlanc, and he made no effort to hide them."

"So it looks as if it wasn't a living, breathing human being who scared the daylights out of us," Leslie said. "How do we know it wasn't an entity? We aren't positive it wasn't, at any rate."

Rose pressed her lips together. She moved closer to Leslie and indicated to Holliday that she wanted him to come near. "It just occurred to me," she whispered, "that someone could be right here in the house with us. Hiding somewhere, biding his time for a chance to turn out the lights and go into the big haunting act." She didn't know why it had taken her so long to come to such a logical conclusion. The house was over a hundred years old and a great deal of wasted space had gone into its construction. At the moment, she could think of several places where someone could hide away without a great amount of discomfort. The narrow closet at the bottom of the stairs, for instance, where she kept the vacuum cleaner and other cleaning equipment because there was no broom closet. There were no convenient places where anyone could remain concealed in the basement but there was an attic, with a flight of steep and narrow stairs from the small door in her bathroom. The storage room on the second floor was another possibility. Still keeping her voice so low no one outside the kitchen could hear, she listed the places where a person with mischief on his mind could hide.

Then she said, "I have a gun, Mr. Holliday. For all we know, we're playing games with a maniac, and I can't imagine going back to bed until every nook and cranny in this house is searched."

Holliday wouldn't let her get the gun from her room but he said her idea was logical, and he would start at the top of the house and work down.

"Not alone," Rose said firmly. "The three of us will stay together, just in case."

An hour later, just as the clock on the living room mantle chimed three, they trouped into the living room, frustrated with defeat. They had searched each room of the house thoroughly, including the attic, and they'd made a return trip to the basement and found no one, not even a place where anything looked disturbed. Rose covered a yawn and suggested they go back to bed. "I'd rather contend with a ghost than a flesh and blood intruder who stalks around trying to frighten people, and I feel safer now that we've looked in every conceivable hiding place and didn't find anyone."

Leslie nodded. Rose noticed how her niece's eyelids were drooping. "I'm practically asleep on my feet, but Aunt Rose—I'm not ashamed to admit I'm afraid to be in my bedroom alone."

"Then you'll finish out the night in my room," Rose answered. "There's the sofa in the bay window that makes into a bed, you know."

Leslie smiled tiredly. "I'll just take off the cushions and throw a blanket or two on it instead of making it out. I'm so tired I could sleep on a bed of nails right now."

Although Rose doubted if she could close her eyes for the few hours that remained of the night, she drifted off into slumber at once, comforted by Leslie's presence every bit as much as Leslie was grateful to be in the room with her. When she awakened and looked out the window the sun was brilliant on the snow. Sometime between the hours of three o'clock when they went to bed and nine when she awakened, the sky had cleared.

She smiled at the sight of the birds flocking around the feeders, a sign that Mrs. Hanson was in the kitchen and wondering when anyone would be down for breakfast. The cook always fed the birds after she came to work in the morning. For a moment, Rose lingered at the window, admiring the vivid blue sky and the colorful plumage of the birds. A small patch of crimson in the snow attracted her attention and she smiled, delighted because she took the bright red movement for a cardinal. But when she looked again, she drew in her breath sharply, and felt the color drain from her face. Dark green leaves were clearly outlined against the dazzling white, and the barely discernible movement she'd seen moments earlier was probably created by stirrings of the light wind. The wind had all but stopped around two or three o'clock, but now she could see the snowy branches of the trees lightly swaying, so the wind could easily have moved the two long-stemmed roses in the snow as well. She blinked her eyes and opened them again, expecting the roses to disappear before her eyes since she'd obviously imagined them. But no, they were still there, bright red against the pristine white. As if they'd been carelessly dropped, then left to shrivel in the wintry blast.

Rose slipped into the blue velvet gown she had worn during the long and frustrating night, put on bedroom slippers and ran down the stairs. In the dining room, she looked out the window and the roses were just as they had been. Impossible, because they couldn't be there. But they were, unless she was losing her mind. She opened the kitchen door and breathed in the rich fragrance of freshly made coffee, aware of the relief that rolled over her when she saw Mrs. Hanson putting strips of bacon in a skillet. She licked her dry lips and forced herself to speak in a normal tone. "Good morning. It looks as if the snow storm is over."

Mrs. Hanson turned from the stove and smiled. "It's a pretty day, too, but my! It's turned awful cold and that wind just cuts through a person like a knife. I figured you'd be coming down to breakfast pretty soon. me and Hanson already had ours and he's down there in the basement trying to get the furnace to put out more heat."

Rose went to the kitchen window. By pressing her face to the window pane and looking out of the corners of her eyes, she could barely see the roses. "Mrs. Hanson, has anyone come to visit this morning?"

"Lands no, Mrs. Winter. Hanson limped around to the front of the house and took a look at the road. Why, there's a big snowdrift down a ways that's higher than any car. It'll be a long time before anyone can get to this house unless they've got a helicopter. I suppose maybe if a person had snow shoes they'd be able to make it if they wanted to bad enough. Like Mr. David Dedrick, for one. But me and Hanson had a real hard time just getting to the house from the cottage."

Rose closed her eyes and wondered why the snow around the roses had not be disturbed. Not a single footprint indented the snow. Then she wondered if they had fallen from the sky. Or were tossed from a plane passing over.

"Why did you ask, ma'am? Was you expecting somebody?"

"No, I—um, when I first woke up, I thought I heard the doorbell ring," Rose improvised. "But I was probably dreaming."

"Here's your coffee," Mrs. Hanson said. Rose turned and lifted the cup from the table, wondering how she could go about asking Mrs. Hanson to look out the dining room window without telling her why she wanted her to.

The birds would make a fine excuse. "I saw a strange bird," she said. "It was near the evergreens under the dining room window. Maybe it's still there and you can tell me what kind it is."

"Well, if it's still there, maybe I can," the cook said as she went into the dining room. "My daddy used to tell me about all the different birds when I was a youngun, back in Indiana, but I don't know too much about Nevada birds."

Rose trailed after her, holding her coffee cup in one hand and holding her breath, hoping Mrs. Hanson would exclaim over the startling sight of hot-house roses in the snow. Instead, she stood at the window, looked out, and said, "Why, I don't see anything but a few chickadees and sparrows. Those little white-throated ones. Maybe it flew away.

What color was it?"

"Red—something like a cardinal, sort of, but more of a rose red."

"Well, maybe it'll come back." Mrs. Hanson trotted to the kitchen, muttering about the frying bacon. "If you see it again, Mrs. Winters, just give a holler. You want me to make cheese omelets for breakfast, I guess, with bacon and orange juice."

"Yes," Rose said faintly as she looked out the window and saw nothing but a few birds and snow stretching endlessly into the distance.

V

During breakfast, Allan Holliday said he would
check out the wiring in the house, but first he felt he
should remove the heavy accumulation of snow
from the driveway. Rose protested, but Holliday
insisted, reminding her that Mr. Hanson was not
able to do the job. Even if the sun stayed out and
some of the snow melted, it would be better to have
the driveway cleared because not all the snow would
melt and it would soon be Monday morning, with
the necessity of getting Leslie into Carson City.

Leslie said she would help, but as soon as Holliday
was out of hearing distance Rose took her aside and
spoke in a voice that reminded Leslie of cloak-and-
dagger operations.

"The most dreadful notion occurred to me. What
if it's Mr. Holliday who wants my house?"

"You can't be serious, Aunt Rose."

"Now, Leslie, I've been doing a lot of thinking. In
the first place, I never heard the eerie voice until he
came to the house. Oh, I know you and Mrs. Hanson

are convinced there's a real ghost on the premises, but I've never felt that way. Now that I think about it, he was almost too conveniently on the spot, you know?''

Leslie looked at her aunt and shook her head. "No, I don't know! What on earth are you talking about?''

Rose flung her arms out wide. "I'm talking about him being there in the parking lot at a time when you needed a Good Samaritan, that's what. I mean —how do we know your car trouble wasn't something he manufactured, and then, after he got here, the disturbances were caused by him. With the aid of some clever mechanical devices that are available at most stores, almost anyone can make voices come or go at will, turn off lights—''

"But he—Aunt Rose, he's Allan *Holliday*. A famous and probably wealthy man who—''

Rose smiled triumphantly, and Leslie could see her fertile imagination at work. "How do we know for sure he's Allan Holliday? What if he's just pretending to be?''

"But Aunt Rose, I know he's who he says he is. I've been introduced to him, he's been working on his picture series for several days—''

"Of course you were introduced to him. But anybody can pawn himself off as someone else. How about that man who goes around imitating and pretending to be that writer—I can't think of his name just now, but surely you've read about him.''

"Yes, but—''

Rose continued, twisting her hands as she paced around the room. "Have you ever seen a picture of Allan Holliday, for instance?''

"No, but the Governor—''

"The Governor is a human being just like the rest of us and not above making a mistake. For all we know, this man is an impostor. He may have done away with the real Allan Holliday, strangled him and shoved his body in a shallow grave on the desert. We don't know what he has on his mind. He could be an escaped mental patient with some diabolical scheme up his sleeve and getting ready to carry it out. I just can't forget how very convenient it was for him to be right there, Johnny-on-the-spot, when you couldn't get your car started. How do you know he didn't do something to it beforehand, to keep it from starting?"

"Oh, Lord, Aunt Rose, don't let your imagination carry you away. You're not writing a book, you know. He—" Leslie dropped her eyes and closed her mouth.

"He *what?*" Rose looked at her niece expectantly. "Well, what were you going to say about him?"

Leslie shook her head. "I wasn't going to say anything about him. Something flashed through my mind when you were talking and it was important, but I can't remember what it was. But it had nothing to do with Mr. Holliday's identity. Please, Aunt Rose, don't allow your creative mind to dwell on the possibility that we're harboring an impostor. I've seen him taking pictures all over the place, and . . . well, I'm sure he's who he says he is, that's all."

Leslie put on a bright blue ski outfit, a white fake fur parka and matching mittens, then struggled into her boots before she went outside. The icy air stung her face so she took the ski mask from her pocket and put it on before she began shoveling. Holliday smiled at her, but said nothing until they'd worked

69

steadily for a few minutes. Then he gestured toward the northern sky where sullen black clouds roiled ominously. The wind had turned wild, strong enough to mold and outline Leslie's figure under her ski pants and jacket.

"We'd better hurry if we're going to get this job finished before its starts coming down again" Holliday yelled above the wind. "Those clouds that're building up look as black as tornado breeders."

Leslie nodded and shoveled faster. The sun was no longer shining and it seemed to her the temperature, bitter cold to begin with, had dropped several degrees during the short time she'd been outside. She worked steadily, and except for her mittened hands and her toes, she was almost uncomfortably hot under the ski clothes. Holliday was making steady progress too. They had cleared a path all the way to the end of the driveway just as Mitch LeBlanc's snow plow came majestically but noisily up the hill, spewing several feet of snow on both sides of the road. Mitch shut off the engine and climbed down from his rig, his breath coming out of his mouth in white puffs as he greeted them:

"Real bad new storm brewin'. Thought I better get the road cleared before it dumps down several more inches, seein' that you'll be wantin' to get on back to wherever you're stayin' at, Holliday. If I was you, I wouldn't wait around another minute because if you don't get out while the gettin's good, you could be stuck here for several days."

"I promised Mrs. Winters I'd check out her wiring before I leave," Holliday answered.

Mitch stamped his feet, remarking that he had poor circulation, and took off his gloves so he could light a cigar. "Hell, I could do that for her. No trick

70

at all. I got all the equipment I need, all I have to do is go back to the house and get it."

"Mrs. Winters has a Voltmeter," Holliday said. "That's about all I need, and I'm sure you're taking care of a much greater need by clearing off the road."

"Oh, hell yes, but somebody's got to do it. You depend on them damn county fellas, you might as well hold out your hand and whistle Dixie. The wife is poorly, you know, but it don't make no difference to them dudes that work for the country whether a man has got an invalid wife or not. Nothin' matters to them, savin' for coffee breaks and vacation time. They never come out here and clean the snow off the county roads. But I heard tell they got it all off of the highway."

Holliday frowned at the dirty ridge of snow that lay across the driveway, courtesy of Mitch LeBlanc. "Leslie, it's getting colder by the second, and you look frozen. I'll just clear away the place where the blades put a mound of snow across the driveway we just cleaned, then I'll be right in." He gave LeBlanc a bland smile. "I'm sure your neighbor wants to get back to his sick wife as quickly as possible."

"This-here is what they call popcorn snow," Mitch said as Allan Holliday's remark sailed right over his head. He hoisted himself back behind the wheel and said, "Fine for anybody foolish enough to want to ski, but the devil's own chore to scrape off the roads. I tell you, there's a glaze of ice underneath it a couple inches deep. I know it's none of my business, Holliday, but if I was you I sure would get out while it's safe."

"How is Veronica today, Mitch?" Leslie looked up at Mitch's face as she spoke, amused at the sullen

71

set of his mouth and jaw. Watching the two men reminded her of a couple of male dogs downwind of a bitch in heat, but she would never voice such a thought, especially to her aunt.

Mitch looked down at her and grinned. "Well, I tell you. Right now she's feelin' just real good. Funny the way it strikes Veronica, sort of like it comes in waves. Be up and around in the wheel chair one minute, bright and chipper as you please, then the next thing you know she's down in the bed and sick as a poisoned puppy. She seen your young man go by earlier on, Leslie. Had his snowshoes on, looked to Veronica like he was headin' for up in town. Could of waited a bit, then he could of drove in, because he knows I always clear off the roads, but I guess maybe he was in a hurry. His folks probably needed a little something from the grocery store. Them Dedricks, they never was provident. Now, you take a family that's been here through one cold season, they ought to learn real quick to keep a supply of canned goods and powdered milk on hand, plenty of makin's for light bread and biscuits. But them Dedrick's never give a thought to the winter comin' on. You'd think they would have more sense. Ever since before Nevada was a state they's been Dedricks in Virginia City and they was all borned here, even David's mom. They set such a store by an education, makin' sure all the younguns get to college and like that, you'd think they'd know when a storm is brewin'. Well, they's bright folks and they's average ones like me, then they's educated fools, and them Dedricks fall in the last category. Takes all kinds, though."

Holliday made short shrift of the snow that Mitch's plow had piled across the driveway and

Leslie was glad enough to go inside. She had reached the front porch when Holliday called her, his face showing inner alarm. She ran back to where he was standing and looked in the distance toward where he was pointing. "Smoke," he said. "What a terrible tragedy. The fire fighting equipment could never get here in time to save that house by the looks of the smoke."

Leslie almost burst into relieved laughter. "That's not smoke, it's just the steam rising from the ground over by the ruins of the Thurston Overstock house. During extremely cold weather it looks like smoke. It's probably not any more than usual, but because of the extremes in temperature, there always seems to be a lot more of it during the cold months."

"Good Lord!" Holliday carried his shovel as he walked with Leslie toward the house. "I should think it would be dangerous. Like Mt. St. Helens, for instance, that caused so much damage. Surely there's a hot-bed of lava down there, just waiting to erupt."

"Well, it's never blown yet," Leslie said. "And there's no history of any eruption, either. It's not a volcano, just a hot spring down deep in the ground."

"Too bad all that energy can't be trapped, then, and put to good use," Holliday mused as they entered the house. "I would guess that steam is rising a half-mile into the sky. If I were your aunt, I certainly would find someone to tap into the hot springs for heating as she's already planned. I had no idea the springs were so enormous, though."

The wind turned even more vicious, but during the time Holliday traced out the wiring in the house no more snow fell. By noon he had examined the complete circuit, but found nothing suspicious, nothing that could account for the capricious way the lights sometimes went out. After a thorough check of the big fuse box on the enclosed back porch, he frowned and shook his head. Leslie had come with him because he'd asked her to. "Nothing. I don't understand it, but no one is perfect. It's possible that I've overlooked something. Now, how about letting me show you the important things to know about this console?"

"I'm afraid of electricity," she said truthfully. She'd already told him she didn't know a circuit breaker from a hat pin.

"There's nothing to be afraid of. Your aunt is one of the most feminine women I've ever met, but she knows how to cut off the current, how to turn off the power to the stove and water pump. Some day you may be alone in the house and it's always best to be prepared."

"Prepared for what?" Leslie laughed uneasily to cover her creepy feeling at actually touching the dangerous looking black things that contained so much power. "You sound like a Scoutmaster, instructing a Girl or Boy Scout."

"Ready for anything. For instance, what if Mrs. Hanson spills cooking oil on the stove? The best way to make sure a fire of that nature doesn't spread is to cut off the power to the stove. There's the electric pump, too, that supplies the house with water. People are accustomed to turning a faucet and getting an abundant supply of water. Out here in the country, I'm sure there's no water service from town, and anything with movable parts can go haywire. A man could come out from town to repair the pump if it should stop working, but someone in the house should know how to turn the power off so the repairman wouldn't get electrocuted, and be able to turn it on if he should signal that he wanted to test it. If you run out of water it might be no fault of the pump, on the other hand. The well could go dry, and if that happens it's important to turn off the pump because a few minutes of pumping air instead of water can ruin a piece of equipment that cost several hundred dollars."

"Okay. Just show me what to do." No cold on earth was as penetrating as the inside of an unheated back porch, she decided, enclosed as that one was, or not.

Holliday pointed out the neatly printed cards that had been glued to each switch. "The one at the top shuts off everything. That's the main switch. Flip it to the right and there's no electrical power in the house." Quickly, he ran his index finger down both sides of the console, pointing out the circuit breakers for the electric range, the water pump, the central air conditioning unit. "The rest are clearly marked too," he said. "This portion provides juice to the outlets in the downstairs part of the house— living room, dining room and so on. The other side takes care of the upstairs rooms."

Leslie nodded. "I think I understand it." She turned and almost tripped over a broken floor tile. Most of the back porch floor was in a bad state of repair and very few of the tiles were intact. They probably disintegrated because of the unrelenting coldness, she supposed. "It was a dumb thing to do, to put tile on a back porch," she remarked.

Holliday broke her fall and she thanked him. He turned around for a second and looked back toward the fuse box just as they went into the kitchen, but

Leslie wasn't going to go back for another lesson, or a test of her memory, she decided, if he asked. He didn't ask, and she stood for a moment in front of the stove where Mrs. Hanson had a big kettle of chicken and noodles simmering on the back burner, grateful for the warmth.

"Lunch in five minutes," the cook said. "Mrs. Winters is setting the table."

"I appreciate the invitation," Holliday said, "but I can't stay if I want to get away before the roads become impassable again."

"Too late," Mrs. Hanson replied as she deftly flipped a tossed salad from a stainless steel bowl into a crystal one. "Leslie, if you'll take the salad dressing to the table, I'll appreciate it. I made three kinds. And Mr. Holliday, if you wouldn't mind bringing the biscuits, it'd help. They're in that basket, with a napkin over them." She gestured with her head toward the basket while she poured chicken and noodles into a bowl.

Holliday carried the biscuits to the table, but he refused to stay. The fresh snow had begun to fall, but he was sure his four-wheel drive would make it, he said, and he needed to get back into Reno. From lowered eyelashes, Leslie watched her aunt playing the part of the gracious hostess, protesting because the guest was going to leave before lunch.

Rose wore a soft beige wool sweater with a white lace collar and a pair of coral colored slacks, and looked almost as young as Leslie. Her appearance and demeanor, as well as her speaking voice and words, made it almost impossible for Leslie to believe she had spoken those earlier doubts about Allan Holliday being an impostor. He thanked her for her hospitality and she insisted that she was more grateful than she could ever say for his bringing Leslie home safely the night before, and for doing so many things for them. He looked at her and smiled, his eyes giving away his private feelings, and she insisted that he come back again, and soon; hopefully they would have no more foolish occurrences. She told him she was extremely relieved that he'd found nothing wrong with the wiring and thanked him again. After he was in his four-wheeler, Rose stood at the window, waving and smiling while Leslie hoped the food didn't get too cold to eat.

She expected Rose to turn around with a sign of relief and say something to the effect that she was glad Mr. Holliday had left. Instead, Rose Winters sat down, wiped her eyes with a lace-edged handkerchief and said, "Dear me, I can't believe myself. I'm really quite—well—" She blushed, cast an uneasy glance at Leslie and took a bite of salad. "I must say, he certainly grows on a person."

Leslie swallowed a bite of scrumptuous chicken before she spoke. "But earlier you were doubting he was the real Alan Holliday!"

"That was just because—well, yes. I did have a few doubts, but that was only my imagination, combined with not enough sleep." Rose helped herself to the chicken and dimpled, her blue eyes shining. "Besides, I must say it's rather ridiculous for a woman of my age to get—not exactly a crush, but—you know."

"You're only thirty-six," Leslie said. "Good Lord, Aunt Rose, people can fall in love at any age."

Rose's voice crackled and she enunciated each word with great care. "I didn't say I was in *love* with him, Leslie."

She toyed with her food, as if concentrating on the

way the noddles curled around the fork. Addressing herself to the plate, she murmured, "What I feel for him is likely a silly schoolgirl crush. Maybe more like an infatuation, when I'm not wondering if he was behind the weird events. But honestly, Leslie, I don't really think he wants my house. I can't imagine why I should even have come up with anything so foolish."

"Obviously someone does, Aunt Rose," Leslie stated. Then she smiled. "Unless we're being visited on a regular basis by an authentic being from the Great Beyond. Aren't you going to eat anything aside from a couple of bites of salad?"

"Oh, yes. Oh, dear." Rose looked utterly confused, and every bit as charming. She arose from her chair and ran to the window. "I thought I heard Mr. Holliday's vehicle coming into the driveway."

Leslie hadn't heard a thing but the howling wind, but she reminded herself that she wasn't twittering around about a man the way her aunt was.

Holliday came in with snow-covered shoulders and a face that was reddened by the wind. "Is your offer still standing, Rose? The State Highway Department has closed off all the roads. I should have left sooner."

"Oh, Allan!" Rose clasped her hands under her chin and fluttered her long, golden eyelashes and managed to look so much like the star in an old-fashioned melodrama that Leslie had to turn her head. "Of course the offer is still open!"

Nothing unusual happened throughout the afternoon. Holliday spent most of his time reading, Rose worked on her book, and Leslie worked on a full-length robe she was embroidering for her mother's birthday. The dressing gown itself was fashioned simply, and made of cotton, but the finished item would be worth a small fortune. Completed, it would be elaborately beautiful because from top to bottom, and including both long sleeves, it would be embroidered in the three silken shades of blue Leslie had chosen. A year previously they'd visited a museum in San Francisco where a similar garment adorned a statue of a fifteenth century Chinese Empress. She was just finishing a dramatic bird-in-flight that would decorate the back when the front doorbell rang. Since she had been expecting David Dedrick throughout most of the day, Leslie put down her work and went to the door.

To her surprise, Doctor Kellerman greeted her. "Come in," she said, "good heavens, how in the world did you make it up the hill?"

"In my sleigh," answered the doctor. He swept the snow from his boot and Leslie brushed most of it away from the shoulders of his coat. "I had to deliver a baby on the outskirts of town. Just like in the old days, Leslie, when there wasn't any hospitals available for most of the folks around these parts. Since I was already out in this blasted weather, I decided to check on Veronica LeBlanc. Tried to call them, but like most folks, they don't have any telephone service. Then I figured I might be able to beg a spot of hot buttered rum from your lovely aunt before I face the long cold ride back into town."

Doctor Kellerman had a melodious speaking voice and in spite of his sometimes flowery phrases, he never sounded as if he were play-acting. He was born and had brown up in a small New England town, spoke five languages and often dined with the Governor and other heads of state, but he was just as much at home with his feet under the kitchen table of a construction worker as he was at the Governor's Mansion.

"Sounds delicious," Leslie said. "I'll go out to the kitchen and make them myself. Mrs. Hanson is over at the cottage with her husband. She has dinner in the oven, but she's a little worried about him."

"I imagine his arthritis is giving him a hard time again."

Kellerman looked at her near-sightedly as he wiped the steam from his glasses. "Perhaps I'd best stop over to the cottage after I've enjoyed a little libation to get my blood warm. Arthritis is usually excruciating."

"Is that what it is?" Leslie took him into the family room. "Mrs. Hanson says he's down in his back."

Her aunt left her desk and rose to greet the doctor with her customary grace, then began to introduce him to her guest, but Doctor Kellerman and the photographer had met shortly after Holliday arrived at the State Capitol.

While she was making hot buttered rum for the two men, pouring sherry for her aunt and fixing herself a cup of coffee, Leslie wondered why Allan hadn't said a word about knowing Doctor Kellerman when Mitch LeBlanc referred to him. It was strange of him to let the poor fool rattle on like that when all the time the two of them had enjoyed dinner at the Governor's Mansion when Holliday first came to town. Come to think of it, Rose had mentioned something about Doctor Kellerman too, and Allan didn't indicate he was already acquainted with the doctor. Oh well, the way she'd rattled on herself about Doctor Kellerman having a thing for her aunt, she supposed Allan didn't actually have an opportunity to say anything, and anyway, it wasn't of great importance. When she came back to the family room the doctor's handsome grey head was inclined toward Holliday and his expression was rapt, while Rose looked slightly uncomfortable.

"How very fortunate you were to be here at a time like that, my dear fellow," Kellerman was saying. "I would give a considerable price to be in on something of that nature."

"But Doctor Kellerman," Rose was saying, "we've just explained that we're pretty sure it's a hoax."

The doctor raised his eyebrows. "You also said Allan has checked out the wiring from basement to attic and found nothing amiss, my dear Rose. No cause for your pecular blackouts, in other words, but at the same time you've explained that there was electricity in the cottage, also down the hill at the LeBlancs' and the Dedricks'."

Rose thanked Leslie for the small glass of sherry and the two men looked at one another in the unmistakable manner of men who are smitten with the same woman but have made up their minds to be civilized.

"Delicious, Leslie," Kellerman said. He looked into the fireplace, his dark brown eyes inscrutable, while Rose explained that Holliday had figured out a way the voice could have been projected into the entire house. When she had finished, he nodded. "I appreciate your logical mind, Rose."

"Most of the time," Rose said, "when uncanny occurrences take place, there's a perfectly reasonable cause."

"Yes, but I can't go along with—of course, it's

very unscientific of me, I'm sure. A psychic phenomenon might be put to severe tests before one can leap to the conclusion that there's been one. But don't you see, Rose, you have the perfect laboratory for testing! The Hansons are probably the most unlikely couple in the entire world to commit chicanery. I can't think of anyone more stolid, even dull, than Jim Hanson, and while Mary is a fine woman and an excellent cook, she has no imagination. Mary Hanson believes the place is haunted. She's *convinced!* On top of that, you've been lucky enough to have a nationally known man in the house during the time these events have occurred. Granted, an unknown person could have crept into your furnace room and called out the well known phrase that has long been said to be audible in this house at times. The same unknown person just as easily could have caused your lights to go out. But how? There's now on the ground, which would certainly show that someone had been walking about in it, and you've already said there was no one in the basement when you went down to search.''

"I don't believe that voice came from the dead and that's all there is to it," Rose said.

"But I'll bet a hundred dollars you were immensely relieved when Allan was turned back because the roads have been closed." Kellerman finished his drink and smiled. "Rose, I'll up my offer if you'll reconsider selling the house."

"I don't want to sell," Rose said with a definite lift of her firmly molded chin. "I like it here and I don't intend to allow some madman to cause me to leave it."

The doctor walked toward the door saying he'd go over to the cottage and Rose offered him another drink. He said he would enjoy another one before he left in the sleigh. When he came back, he accepted the hot drink but didn't refer again to his offer to buy the house. The doctor did remark about the bulging tile on the back porch. "Since you're obviously snowed in for a few days, Allan, why don't you do something about it? We don't need to risk having someone fall, and it seems to me the icy blast will ruin a few more tiles back there. I found a hammer on the floor near the door and pounded the one that was broken to smithereens, then swept them up. But that's temporary, at best."

Allan said he would take care of it, and Doctor Kellerman left, the tinkling sleigh bells audible long after the sleigh was out of sight.

After the doctor left, Holliday explained why he hadn't mentioned knowing the doctor when Mitch LeBlanc was there. "The man is openly hostile to me, and if I said yes, I met him at the Governor's Mansion, I probably would have antagonized him further, and I didn't want to."

After dinner, Rose did the dishes so Mrs. Hanson could be with her husband. Leslie thought about the offending tiles on the back porch, but after darkness fell the temperature of the thermometer outside the dining room window registered thirteen below, and she didn't want to suggest that the photographer go out in the cold to work, even if it would take only a few minutes.

David arrived at seven-thirty, shortly after the disquieting information that had come over the air that the new blizzard had dropped seven inches of snow on Reno, nine in the higher elevations around Virginia City, and no relief was in sight. The Governor appeared on the television screen and spoke gravely, asking everyone to stay off the highways because the emergency equipment wasn't capable of keeping the roads clear and if the snow didn't stop falling, Nevada would be declared a disaster area. A record breaking five-inches of powdery snow had been dumped on Las Vegas, which resulted in several collisions and two deaths. Several accidents had taken place in Reno, many in Carson City. So far the injuries to people were minor, but the vehicles involved were, in most cases, irreparable. Incidents of looting had been reported in downtown Reno and Carson City and the Governor admonished the public tersely: "Unless it's a matter of life or death, I repeat my request to stay off the streets and safely in your homes. If you run out of fuel with which to heat your homes, report it to the police, who will either send someone for you in a vehicle capable of making it through the huge amounts of snow that have piled up on the highways and take you to temporary shelter, or provide you with a temporary supply of fuel. Almost every store in the state has closed. Except for Las Vegas, where the casinos are operating as usual and most of the business places are open, sensible Nevada residents have gone home, gotten off the streets. Law enforcement officers are armed and have orders to shoot if they see anyone forcing entry into any of the business establishments that have closed down because of the heavy accumulation of snow. If you are out of food, if there's sickness in your family, call this emergency number." The Governor slowly intoned the telephone number while it was flashed on the screen for a full minute.

David had arrived quietly on snowshoes, and no one heard him until he rang the bell. He brought a butane camp-style coffee maker and a portable, battery operated radio. His mother was afraid the heavy build-up of snow would soon drag the power lines to the ground and Rose's household would be without means of making coffee except for the fireplace, and the radio was David's idea. They'd already heard the weather forecast on the six o'clock news and he wanted the people on the hill to know what was going on. "Mother is about to come down with a bad case of cabin fever," he said, "and she's worried about me being out in the weather. Her instructions were to either spend the night here or come back home at once, and with her getting more and more nervous because of the accumulation of snow, I'd better go back home right away."

"David, we'd love to have you spend the night," Rose said.

He said he appreciated the offer, but shook his head. "Dad's going to need me to help bring in firewood in case we don't have any power. Our furnace operates on oil, but it won't work without the electric switch that turns it on. How about you folks? Have you plenty of firewood, just in case?"

"Plenty," Leslie assured him. A little over a week ago she had helped Hanson stack an enormous amount of wood near the house.

David took two plastic-wrapped packages out of his back pockets. "If anything goes wrong, use these," he said. The packages contained six sky rockets each, the kind that are generally used to celebrate the Fourth of July. They'll make a hell of an explosion, and they also light up the sky. You'd be better off if you had a CB unit, but I know how you feel about that sort of thing, Rose."

Leslie smiled. Her aunt was eccentric in many

85

areas, but when it came to people driving around with C.B. units in their cars she was almost fanatically opposed because a man engrossed in talking over one had hit her car and totaled it. Fortunately, she wasn't hurt, but since she considered even the telephone an invasion of her privacy, she was adamantly against being at the mercy of someone who wanted to get her on the air and "talk about nothing," as she put it. "The LeBlancs have a C.B. in their house as well as the car," she said. "If anyone in the neighborhood has a problem because of the storm, I'm sure Mitch will be the first one to get help."

David had been in touch with Mitch LeBlanc on the C.B. "Veronica is doing much better since Doctor Kellerman came to see her," he said. He exchanged a meaningful glance with Leslie. "I had an idea old Mitch was going to come up the hill and forcefully carry you all down to his place, so I let him know about the rockets and sort of let him know Mr. Holliday was still here. He was under the impression that you left, sir."

"I did," the photographer said. "But the State Highway Department turned me back. How did you know I came back? I didn't pass your house."

"I saw your four-wheeler in the driveway when I went into town," David explained. He told them only one grocery store was open, but everything else was closed down and the grocery store was getting ready to batten the hatches when he was there. "Virginia City looks like an honest-to-God ghost town," he added. "Nothing is moving and everyone's socked in. Half the residents are already without electricity and I understand it's going to get a lot worse before it gets better."

Remembering Mitch LeBlanc's acid remark about the Dedrick family being improvident, Leslie asked David why he'd gone to the store.

"Because the only way Mother can cope with being house-bound is to make enormous quantities of baked goods. She had six packages of yeast on hand, but she was afraid we'd run out of bread and sweet rolls, so I went in and picked up a dozen extra packages. Right now, she's up to her elbows in Danish pastry, so I'll be bringing some over tomorrow if it's possible to get out of the house."

Although Leslie was sorry to see David go so soon, she understood. She went to the door with him and helped him strap on his snowshoes. When she opened the door for him a blast of frigid air and pelting snow took her breath away. "Take care," she called against the screaming wind. It was terrible out there and a frightening thought hit her. "How will I know you made it safely home?"

"I'll send up a rocket," he said. Then he turned, enveloped her in his arms and kissed her gently, which left her oddly shaken. At the dining room window she stood and peered out at the fierce night, searching through the whirling mass of snow until she saw his silhouette, lean and graceful, as he started down the hill. At that moment, she realized he had turned on a flashlight. It twinkled in the blackness, rising and falling with each swooping step. She watched the tiny light until it disappeared, her hands clenched as her mind conjured up visions of him getting lost in a snowdrift, of him freezing to death before anyone realized he hadn't come home. The telephone in the dining room shone brightly under the light from the chandelier, but the line was dead. She hung it up and again went to the window, where she saw the distant lights of the Dedrick house. Moments later a thunderous sound shook the cold window pane and a brilliant display of magenta, fluorescent blues and greens and dazzling white stars lit up the sky. It wasn't until the shower of fireworks came after the explosion that Leslie caught a full breath, and on her way back to the family room she admitted to herself for the first time that she loved him.

VI

Rose had the Scrabble board on the game table when Leslie came back to the family room. She was standing in the middle of the room, frightened. "Leslie, did you hear that dreadful sound? It was loud as a clap of thunder, and I was sure the lights would go out, but they didn't even flicker."

"David shot off a rocket when he reached home," Leslie said.

"Thoughtful of him," commented Holliday.

Rose looked at Leslie and nodded. "David is a thoughtful person. But I wish you'd given me a little warning." She had made up her mind not to try to push Leslie into a relationship she didn't want, but she was a keen observer and was pleased to see a new kind of sparkle in her niece's eyes that made her wonder if Leslie had at last begun to realize how exceptional a young man David was. There was no doubt in Rose's mind that Leslie's relationship with Phillip had been damaging, but it was good to see the girl's natural personality coming out again, and

Rose was confident that David Dedrick was responsible. "Allan and I are going to play Scrabble. How about you, Leslie?"

"I'll get trounced as usual when I play with you, Aunt Rose, but it's fun. Sure, I'll play."

For over an hour the three of them concentrated around the Scrabble board, and Rose kept score. Allan had told her he'd played the game only a few times before, but he was an excellent strategist and took a back seat to no one when it came to presenting unusual words. At the end of the game Rose was ahead of Allan by only five points, with Leslie coming in third, but it had been a close and invigorating game. The lights dimmed a few times, went off once but came back on within seconds, and everyone was relieved. Leslie went to the kitchen to make some popcorn, which she served with some hot spiced cider, but she didn't want to play another game. "I'm into a book I'd like to finish," she said, "and just in case the lights do go off, I'll turn on everyone's electric blanket now so the beds will be warm."

Rose watched her niece leave the room with some qualms. In spite of enjoying every minute she spent with Allan Holliday, she didn't feel quite right about being alone with him. Even so, she was glad to play another game of Scrabble with him. He won by fifty-seven points after playing all seven of his tiles, and Rose was sincere when she congratulated him in spite of being a trifle surprised. It was seldom that Mark was able to beat her at any word game, she remembered. Words were, after all, her forte. But still and all, Allan had won fair and square and she appreciated his thoughtfulness when he said he would go over to the cottage and make sure Mr.

Hanson and his wife were all right before he turned in. She watched him from the back door, his flashlight spilling a great round glow all over the snow. The door of the cottage opened and a square of bright light was visible for a second before he stepped inside.

Rose frowned when she looked at the porch floor. First thing in the morning, she would have to do something about those broken tiles. With them raised up like that and sharding off, they were hazardous, and Mrs. Hanson would probably be the one to trip and fall since she was inclined to stumble where most people didn't. A broken leg or hip would be bad at any time, but worse at a time like this. When she first moved into the house she was aware of the loose and crumbling tiles on the back porch floor, but so many other things had needed renovating that she kept putting it off. Every winter a few more bulged up and broke. Well, she would make a note to herself to take care of it as soon as the winter was over. It wasn't likely that she'd be able to find someone willing to come out and work in the cold.

Something was making a rattling noise against the porch windows, something loud enough to be heard in spite of the howling wind. Rose stepped out into the frigid enclosure and saw that the windows were covered with sleet. When Allan came back it glistened in his hair.

"Just what we needed," he said as they hurried into the warm kitchen. "A sleet storm on top of all that snow! But Mr. Hanson is feeling better. Doctor Kellerman gave him a different kind of medication for his arthritis and he says it's relieved him of most of the pain. By the way, what's Mrs. LeBlanc's problem? Everyone speaks of her as an invalid, but no one says what's wrong with her.''

It was on the tip of Rose's tongue to remark that a good portion of Veronica LeBlanc's illness was probably due to her hard-nosed, embittered husband, but she seldom allowed herself to verbalize her feelings about that sort of thing.

Instead she said, "She had to have a kidney removed because of cancer, but that was several years ago and the other one is apparently functioning very well. She goes to have her checkups twice each year, but there's been no sign of the cancer spreading. Before she was completely recovered from the kidney operation, though, Mitch took her to Reno to do some shopping. She'd been released from the hospital but didn't feel quite well enough to drive. A truck hit them on a curve. Mitch suffered a few cuts and bruises, but Veronica's spine was injured and the first prognosis was frightening—the doctors said she'd never recover from the state she was in, which was total paralysis from the neck down. A few weeks later they concluded she was a good risk for spinal surgery and the operation was fifty percent successful. She could move from the waist up. Her daughter flew here from New Hampshire in order to be with Veronica until Mitch could find suitable help, but the DC-10 she was on collided with a light plane and there were no survivors. When Veronica learned of the tragedy, she went into a deep depression because she felt responsible. You see, if she hadn't needed someone to help take care of her after her surgery, her daughter wouldn't have been on that plane. Anyway, she was never able to walk again.''

Rose was not going to say anything about Mitch's

implications that Veronica could walk if she wanted to, that he suspected she got out of her wheel chair when he was out of the house. She had nothing to go on but Mitch's statements and she suspected that his viewpoint was colored by his own discontent. To date she had been able to gracefully dodge his unwanted attentions. When he referred to his wife's condition and said Veronica didn't want to walk, that she wouldn't try because she wanted to keep him enslaved, Rose always managed to change the subject.

"Why?" She looked at Allan questioningly. "Why are you asking about Veronica?" She wouldn't have asked if Allan's expression hadn't shown an unusual tenseness, if there hadn't been the look of consternation in his eyes.

They went back into the family room and began to put the Scrabble game away before Allan answered. At last he said: "Mr. Hanson said Veronica might be responsible for the mysterious doings here at your house. Mitch asked him to look in on her about a month ago because he had to go to Reno. Mr. Hanson said she was standing up and looking out the front window when he came up the walk, but when she came to the door she was in her wheel chair. In other words, Mr. Hanson believes she can walk if she wants to."

"But why would Veronica—even if she could walk —why should she want to frighten me away? Besides, there were no fresh tracks in the snow last night. You said so yourself, and I looked."

"Apparently Mitch does a lot of blowing and striking in town. He's sort of let people in Virginia City know how he feels about you, and probably some of the good ladies of the town took it upon themselves to let Veronica know her husband has his eye on another woman.''

Rose felt her cheeks flame. "But I've never encouraged him. That horrible man! He's not in the least appealing to me, and I've let him know it. On top of that, he's married, and even though I know his wife only slightly, I certainly wouldn't go behind another woman's back, and—" She was so enraged she had to swallow before she could go on. "Anyway, why hasn't Hanson said anything to me about that kind of thing being said in town?''

Holliday shrugged. "Who knows? Maybe he thinks you're too delicate and refined. An overly-sensitive writer with all the high-flown temperament usually associated with people in the writing profession. On the other hand, he probably thinks there's nothing to back up Mitch's insinuation and didn't want to hurt you. The thing is, there's very little anyone can do about gossip.''

"Just the same, I find it hard to believe that a woman who keeps to the house, is usually confined to bed or a wheel chair, would be physically able to climb a steep hill on foot during a killer snowstorm just to pretend to haunt a house! Besides, Mitch would have known it if she left their home. And there were no footprints in the snow, either.'' The idea that Veronica or anyone else would go to such lengths to perpetrate a hoax was appalling to Rose.

"A small woman wearing snowshoes wouldn't have made much of an impression in that particular kind of snow. It was powdery and the wind was strong. I understand Veronica LeBlanc doesn't weigh any more than ninety pounds. It would have required a little work on her part to cover the slight tracks she did make but it's a possibility. Then too,

Mitch appeared on your doorstep at a very unusual time of night. He said his wife couldn't sleep, remember? His excuse for showing up here sounded valid enough on the surface. If I remember correctly, he said he saw your lights and wondered if everything was all right. But for all we kow, he might have been awakened when Veronica came in out of the cold and had some reason to doubt her when she said she couldn't sleep. It would be difficult for a woman who is allegedly a helpless invalid to explain why her coat was damp. That is, if he had reason to check it out, and as Hanson says, LeBlanc apparently doubts she's all that sick in the first place. At the same time, it would be unlikely that he'd come here and ask point-blank if you'd seen her. Most husbands and wives go to great lengths to protect their spouses, even those who aren't happy."

"But why on earth would she do it? Aside from the fact that she probably couldn't."

"Jealousy, I suppose. You don't know what goes on inside anyone else's mind. Most of us have a few mental quirks, but we learn to live with them. A woman who seldom gets out of the house could be suffering from all kinds of delusions, and even though I don't know her husband well, he doesn't come off to me as the kind of man who would be easy for anyone to get along with. He's referred to the possibility that she's feigning her illness, that she can walk when she wants to. Maybe he's right, because Hanson swears he saw her standing behind the window, as I said. At one time she may have been so disabled that she couldn't walk, but when she recovered maybe she decided to keep it to herself for reasons of her own. How do you know

Mitch doesn't regale her with tales of the charming Mrs. Winters when he's alone with her? Some men get a lift out of bragging to their wives about other women who find them attractive. If she's a shade unstable, she might have seized on the legendary haunting of Overstock House as a weapon to help drive you out."

During the time he was talking, Holliday put more logs on the fire while Rose tidied up the room. From a reasonable and logical point of view, she realized he made sense about Veronica. Earlier in the day she'd suspected him of being an impostor, with devious plans to drive her out of her house by appearing to help her solve the mystery when all the time he was scheming to drive her over the brink by playing tricks of his own. Long before Doctor Kellerman arrived she'd come to the conclusion that she'd been a victim of her own highly developed imagination, confounded by the eerie sight of roses in the snow that shouldn't have been there. She knew by then he wasn't an impostor because she'd spent an hour in her library where she found a picture of him along with a six-page spread of some fabulous photographs he'd made of a well-known plantation near Atlanta. Earlier, she had considered telling Leslie about the roses, but decided against it because Leslie was already overwrought and she didn't want to add another burden on the shoulders of her beloved niece.

All day long Rose had tried to convince herself she had seen no roses that morning, but she hadn't been successful. Down deep, she knew they'd been there, crimson and beautiful against the snow. Then suddenly they weren't there, because neither she nor Mrs. Hanson saw them. Still, they'd come from somewhere. She was positive they were not a figment of her imagination. She was creative, yes. But her ability to invent plots and carry out the theme of a murder mystery to a satisfactory end didn't cause her to see things that did not exist.

"Allan," she began, planning to tell him about the roses because she liked him and had confidence in him, "Shortly after I came downstairs this morning, I saw—" The lights went off and she gasped, then wailed, "Oh, dear, not again."

"It's undoubtedly the storm," Allan said. "Let's just go on upstairs and get in bed. I'm glad Leslie turned on the electric blankets; they'll be warm if we hurry. It isn't as though we haven't been expecting the power to fail, you know; young Dedrick said half of Virginia City was without power, if you remember. We've been lucky to have power this long."

Rose held her breath, afraid she would hear the plaintive, sometimes sharp and quarrelsome voice ordering Becky to come, but the touch of Allan's hand on her arm was comforting. The room was not in total darkness because the fresh logs Allan had put on the fire were burning brightly enough for her to be able to make out individual pieces of furniture. At the doorway, he flicked off the chandelier so it wouldn't blaze away in an empty room when the lights came back on, then turned on the flashlight.

"Let's look outside first," he suggested. "I doubt if anyone else has any lights, but I want to make sure."

Guided by the circular yellow beam of the flashlight, they made their way to the family room windows and looked down the hill toward the LeBlanc house. Total darkness. In the dining room they looked out toward the Dedrick house and saw no sign of lights coming from the windows there, either. Holliday put the flat end of the flashlight against the window pane, sending the light out into the blackness. Snow slanted furiously across the circle of light, driven by the shrieking wind.

"The sleet didn't last long," he said. "Which is probably a blessing." He shone the light toward the ground and Rose shook her head in dismay. A drift that looked at least six feet high curved gently against his vehicle and another taller drift was piled along the fenceline, obscuring everything under it as it swelled upwards and over in a towering arch.

"Thank God we've plenty of food in the freezer," she said. "It'll be days before we can get out. I've never seen a snowstorm this bad."

"I'll set the alarm on that Big Ben wind-up clock in my room so I can replenish the fire in another hour. Then I'll go downstairs and fill the furnace."

He put his arm around her shoulders and she moved closer to him. "I'm so glad you're here, Allan."

"So am I, but you and Leslie are survivors. You'd make out fine without me. Even so, I'm glad I can do a few things to make being snowbound a little easier, and you're lucky you have a coal furnace that can be fired by hand. Let's go to the kitchen and look out at the thermometer."

Rose giggled. "I'm not so sure I want to know how cold it is." But she went with him because she didn't want to leave the comfort of his side.

"Twenty-one below zero," he said. Then he whistled softly.

"There's not a whisper of truth in that old saying I've heard all my life about it getting too cold to snow."

"I understand it snows in Alaska at fifty below, even colder."

Rose said she'd settle for the outskirts of Virginia City.

Outside her bedroom door, Holliday gave her the flashlight. She looked up at him and smiled, and it was the most natural thing in the world for his lips to meet hers. Several breathless seconds later, she gave him back the flashlight and said she had one in her room. She also had a kerosene lamp, which she planned to read by. When the lights went out she forgot all about her intention of telling Allan about the roses she had either seen or not seen in the snow, but when she came upstairs she remembered a book she had in her bedroom that gave an account of the mining boom days of Virginia City, the famous and infamous and their heirs following the decline. Doctor Kellerman had given it to her shortly after she moved into the house but she had read only the first few pages. As far as anyone knew, Leslie's mother and she were next in line to inherit from the Overstocks and she was sure the bank had been thorough in the investigation; still and all, bank lawyers could have overlooked an heir. They were mere human beings and made mistakes just like everyone else, and Rose knew of several instances where a distgruntled heir had gone to great lengths to acquire property he felt was rightfully his. The idea of someone lurking about with the intention of scaring her away so he could move in was much more appealing than admitting there was a restless ghost causing all the trouble.

As soon as she lit the lamp, she found the book on the shelf where she expected it to be. It was entitled *Silver Kings, Queens and Courtesans,* and the author was Derle Kamp. The inside jacket cover concerned itself with a brief biography of the writer, who was born in Virginia City in 1916, left for Chicago in 1929, then returned to live there for a full year while he was compiling the necessary data for the book. His father was a hard-scrabble miner who finally gave in to his mother's wishes to stop pursuing a far-fetched dream of making a big strike.

"My father died believing there was an undiscovered silver bonanza in the Virginia City region. He was delirious with fever, but the silver was still very much on his mind. His last words to me were to go back, and he tried to tell me where I would strike it rich, but he rambled, referred to the big copper mines in another country, the Lost Dutchman Mine in the Superstition Mountains, and talked about a thick vein of silver under downtown Reno, all of which in his confused state he believed to be Virginia City.

"My father was a Johnny-come-lately. He arrived long after the big strike had been made. The big Comstock lode was depleted and Virginia City was quickly becoming a ghost town. It was inhabited by very few people compared with the teeming masses during the heyday period. Down through the years, however, the romance of the place, the historic scope and background kept calling me back. I didn't expect to strike it rich by working claims that had long ago been exhausted, but I wanted to write about the people who settled here, some of them for a short time, others for the rest of their lives. People with gold or silver fever are a breed unto themselves. They're the compulsive gamblers to end all compulsive gamblers, and those few who became millionaires are far outnumbered by those who barely eked out a living. Even after they acquired their wealth, many of them died bitter and broken, even bankrupt, but they all have a story to tell."

The first chapter presented a colorful background of Storey County, referred to the flora and fauna, the diverse backgrounds of the people who rushed to the area, all of them burning with silver fever in spite of many who settled down in the more secure, if more mundane life, of merchants, bankers, saloon keepers and dance hall girls. Mention was made of the more notorious prostitutes, including the Creole beauty named Julia Bulette and the high-tempered Silver-heels Marlowe who allegedly fought at the drop of a hat.

Apparently Veronica LeBlanc was descended from Mormon stock, Rose realized. No doubt her ancestors helped develop irrigation projects at Franktown, in the Washoe Valley, since her maiden name was Jacobsen and she counted a total of six Jacobsens among those hard-working Mormons who followed in the footsteps of the Indians who had long ago established irrigation ditches from the Truckee River to Carson in order to provide food for their countless young. A Veronica Ledford born in 1867 and married to Arnold Jacobsen (his third living wife) in 1883 could have been Veronica LeBlanc's great grandmother. One of her grandchildren was given the unwieldly name, Livonia Veronica, and the one time Mitch had referred to his mother-in-law he called her "Ma Vonnie." But Rose could find no Jacobsen or any of their descendents in the Virginia City region until Veronica and Mitch came there to live after World War II. According to what Mitch had told her, he met his wife in Yuma, Arizona when he was stationed at a naval base there. At the time, Mitch said she belonged to the Church of the Latter Day Saints, but she no longer was affiliated with any religious group. Mitch was born in Kentucky, she remembered. He told her he had never been out of Kentucky except for a trip into Illinois when he was a small boy until he was drafted into the Service during the second World War.

Nothing there, or if there was, it wasn't on the surface.

Since she had already read a great deal about the illiterate miner, Sandy Bowers, who discovered the famous Comstock Lode, and his equally illiterate wife Eilly, Rose skimmed that part rapidly. She was looking for background material about the Overstock family although she was fascinated when she read intimate details about the lives of some of the other miners who became fabulously wealthy.

Louise Dedrick enjoyed talking about Banker Bill Dedrick, her husband's great-grandfather. "Other people," Louise said once over dinner at Rose's house, "were spoken of as being tight-fisted, but he had a reputation for being able to skin a gnat, cut it in twelve equal pieces and serve it up for Sunday dinner." David's father was never uncomfortable when his wife told stories about skinflint Banker Bill. He thought such tales were hiliarious.

Derle Kamp's book didn't refer to his stinginess when it came to feeding his family, never said one word about his making his wife do her own housework when he could have hired a dozen servants, forcing her to serve six eggs for breakfast when their family consisted of two adults and ten children, or insisting on wearing his shirts inside out when they got dirty in order to save on laundry soap. Kemp did write about Banker Bill's inglorious end, though, and it was word for word the way Louise told it after she'd heard the story from her husband's father:

A number of the men who came to Storey County in their search for silver or gold couldn't read or write. Each day at the end of their labors they were accustomed to bringing their "takings" in to Banker Bill Dedrick, who carefully weighed their dust and nuggets and marked down in a black book exactly how much cash money was on deposit if the men felt safer about leaving their loot in his vault. Many of them didn't. Most of them enjoyed a good dinner at the Bird of Paradise or one of the other great eating houses Virginia City offered, then strolled into the nearest saloon to toss a few drinks and get into a friendly game of cards or dice. As often as not, those who kept their gold or silver in their pockets would lose it before the night was through, but those who left at least a part of their cache with Banker Bill were assured of eating until they panned out a payload or found another vein.

For several years, Banker Bill was meticulous about his accounts. If a man signed an X under his name and the amount of funds the banker entered on his account, he had nothing to worry about. Some managed to put by enough savings to open a saloon of their own, or put a doxie on the street and keep her in style until the cash from her labors began to roll in. A few became merchants and one miner went to Sparks for a year where he studied medicine under a doctor. When he came back to Virginia City he hung out his shingle and did a lot of good for the sick of the area, and every time he met Banker Bill Dedrick on the street he shook hands and always said the same thing, "If it hadn't been for you taking care of my money, I wouldn't be a professional man today."

It isn't clear just how or when Banker Bill decided the miners were unworthy of keeping their total receipts, but according to old Court House records there came a day when four rough-riding, hard-talking, tobacco-spitting miners came into his bank just at closing time and demanded their cash. Bill said he didn't have it on hand. One of the four men said, "Hell, no, you don't, just like you didn't have it on hand last week when Jim Archer came in and asked for a little cash money so he could pay his boarding house bill."

The banker tried to explain that he didn't always keep large sums of money on hand because there was always the danger of being robbed. One of the men said, "Jim Archer, he wasn't wantin' no big sum of money, he was only wantin' five dollars so he could pay Mrs. Leary. What you told him was that he never had no money on deposit in your bank atall, not in any shape, form or fashion. Not in dust, not in nuggets. Told Jim Archer he was always so drunk he wouldn't know his rear end from a piece of boar bacon, he only thought he brought you his takings. Now Bill, we want our money."

Bill did a little dance, then looked up hopefully when the door opened. Probably he would have been glad to see the devil himself come into the bank at that moment, but it was Lydia Parsons, the seamstress. Bill jumped out from behind his little barred window and tried to hide behind pretty Lydia, but his portly body stuck out on both sides of her, making a fine target for four blazing guns. Miss Lydia was some shaken up over the event, but she wasn't really hurt. Banker Bill didn't die of the wounds in his sides, he died of blood poisoning because the proud doctor didn't know anything about washing his hands or taking other antiseptic measures when it came to removing bullets.

A cartoon, copied with permission from the *Territorial Enterprise*, June 11, 1869, depicted the portly little banker hiding behind the skirts of the seamstress while the four guns blazed away.

Most of Banker Bill's descendants were scattered across the country, according to Victor and Louise Dedrick, but they'd preferred to live in Virginia City. The banker wasn't born in the house where David and his parents lived, but one of his sons was, the one who was Victor's grandfather. Like Rose, Louise enjoyed living in a house where history abounded and the house long ago had been restored to its early splendor.

The chapter about the Overstock family told Rose nothing she didn't know, but she was pleased to find a number of marvelous photographs as well as some excellent etchings. One showed Mr. and Mrs. Peter Overstock being helped down from a fancy carriage by a servant. They were outside the entrance of the Piper Opera House. Another one was a stunning full-face painting (copied with permission of the local Historical Society) of Becky Overstock. Her hair was arranged modishly and her dress was elaborate. When Rose saw the three roses the original woman of the house held in her lovely hands she felt her flesh break out in chills, but her eerie feeling was even more pronounced when she saw the picture of the beautiful Becky Overstock in her San Francisco home. The man who was seated on the chair in front of Peter Overstock's widow was Thuston, his brother, although the caption said the man was her husband. Rose was positive it was

Thurston because she had seen several pictures of Thurston. Two were in the book, in fact, so she leafed back and studied them closely. There was no doubt about it. It was Thurston Overstock in the ornate chair, and Becky stood with one hand on his shoulder, the other holding three long-stemmed roses. It *had* to be Thurston, because Peter had been dead for over a year when the photograph was made.

The Overstocks were not members of the Mormon church, so there was no possibility that Thurston had followed in the footsteps of many other good Mormons before him and simply taken another wife. She closed the book after a few more moments of futile searching for another heir to the estate, and there was no doubt in her mind that Becky and Thurston had been lovers. Lovers who may or may not have used the flower always associated with love when sent by a man to a woman, at least back in those days before women began sending flowers to men—but she vowed to not allow herself to get all steamed up about the roses in the snow just because of a coincidence, especially when she wasn't sure she'd seen them in the first place.

The house was quiet. Strangely quiet without the familiar if barely audible sound of the electric clocks, the hushed motor of the refrigerator that wouldn't come on, the non-working controls on the furnace that fed the iron fireman. She wondered if the snow had stopped, but by the time she stretched out full length in the bed she didn't want to look out and see. At any rate, it fell silently.

The last thing she saw before she went to sleep was an image of roses, bright red against a dazzling path of pure white snow.

VII

Leslie awakened abruptly from a pleasant dream. She turned over, pressed her head deeper into the pillow and tried to go back to sleep after a quick look at the pitch black windows, which told her it was still too early to get up. Instead of falling back into slumber her mind began to work at top speed. Impatient with herself, she assumed one more position and willed herself back to sleep, to no avail. After about twenty minutes of lying there with racing thoughts, she slipped into her robe and bedroom slippers and went to the window where she drew in a sharp breath at the sheer beauty of the land. No more than a glimmer of dawn was in the sky, just a faint lightening in the deep blue with a few streaks of pearlescent pink lined in magenta. But there was enough light to illuminate the drifts of snow down below, purple in the shadows, dark lavender where the brightening sky reflected its light. Smaller trees were so heavily laden that they bent to the ground in graceful arches. It reminded her of the low desert where the wind sculptures the sand in intricate patterns that resemble rippling ocean waves just barely blown along by the wind. But there was utter stillness out there. No wind, and although it wasn't light enough for her to see for sure, she didn't think any more snow was falling. The sky grew brighter blue, with gorgeous glowing pinks that changed to fiery cerise and luminescent orange as she stood, transfixed. The purple shadows on the drifts faded to violet, then blue and orchid when the sun first appeared, a narrow crescent of burning red glowing brighter with each passing second. Without a doubt, it was the most sublime sunrise Leslie had ever seen in her life.

The house was warm and since no one else would be up at that ungodly hour, she went downstairs in her robe and put on the coffee. The light didn't come on when she pushed the button on the Mr. Coffee machine, but it took her a while to notice. She poured the water into the top as she always did and went to the back door where she looked out toward the cottage, hoping Mr. Hanson was feeling better. The snow had drifted all the way up beyond the glass in the back door of the enclosed porch, and all the windows were equally covered, so she couldn't see the cottage. After a quick dash into the dining room she was relieved to see it was actually a twelve or fourteen foot drift of snow at the back of the house instead of that much of an accumulation as she had first feared. Looking out the windows of the dining room, she saw that a minimum of sixteen or eighteen inches had fallen through the night, but the drifts were a sight to behold. The birds were congregating around the feeders, but most of the seed was gone.

When she went back to the kitchen to get sunflower seed and the other ground grain, she noted that the red light on the coffee machine wasn't on. "Hmmm," she said, looking at the pale amber fluid that dripped into the glass server. A touch of her hand against the coffee maker was enough to tell her it was cold even if the anemic looking brew that fell into the glass container hadn't been a clue. The interior refrigerator light didn't come on when she opened the door, either. Then she noticed that the electric clock on the range had stopped at five minutes after eleven, which meant the electricity had been out all night long.

"First things first," she muttered, then put on her boots and a heavy coat so she could go out andd fill the bird feeders, using the side door where there were no drifts. They were swooping down with a great flutter of wings and glad cries of gluttony before she was able to slog her way back to the house.

Welcome warmth came up the basement steps when she went back into the house. If she could figure out how to work the butane burner David had brought the day before she would make coffee on it. If not, she decided to boil some in the fireplace, campfire style. It would blacken the pan, of course, but the prospect of scrubbing soot off the bottom of a pan was far more appealing than going without her morning coffee, and she had always been afraid of mechanical contrivances that worked on gas. To her it was as frightening as fooling around with electricity.

After she took off her coat and boots and brushed the snow from the bottom of her robe she looked at butane tank, read the instructions, and touched the shiny knob, imagining herself striking a match to the deadly looking burner after she had turned the knob to the "on" position. She knew she could never force herself to do it. She put the burner back and took an aluminum pan from the pantry, regretful about the shiny surface but filled it with water to the brim. She was halfway into the family room where she had no doubt Allan Holliday had kept a fire going through the night when she realized the entire house was warm. Which meant the furnace was functioning, a furnace with a nice flat surface on the top that would bring the water to a boil in a few minutes.

Without hesitating, she went down the basement steps, muttered "Darn!" because she'd turned the switch at the top of the stairs out of habit. It made a clicking sound, but no light came on and the basement was as black as the inside of a cave because of the snow that covered all the windows. Just knowing it was dark because of the snow against the windows didn't settle her growing sense of anxiety. For a second or two, she stayed where she was. On the fourth step from the top she remembered the flashlight she should have brought down with her. Then she saw a reassuring glow of brightness from the vicinity of the furnace room and talked herself into going down the remaining steps, confident that she could muddle her way through the task she had set for herself without going back upstairs.

The furnace room was faintly illuminated from the burning coals inside. They showed brightly through the open draft and around the edges of the door, providing enough light for Leslie to put the pan of water on top. It made a sizzling sound because she'd spilled a little water, but it pleased her because it meant the water would boil soon. Wasting no time, she sprinted toward the dark and cavernous stairway, tripped over the first step, but didn't fall all the way, righted herself and felt around for it, more cautious since she could have hurt herself. While she groped with her right foot for the step something ran across her left one. She froze, held her breath and listened, too paralyzed with fear to move for a second. Mouse? Water-bug? Whichever, she couldn't stand down there forever with one foot on the first step, the other waiting for the bite of a mouse's teeth or a nibble from a bug's jaw, if that's what the loathsome things did. "Oh, God," she breathed, and forced herself to feel along the wall as she mounted the steps. It was then she heard the scraping sound from the laundry room and screamed. She kept it up until she was safely at the top of the stairs and bursting through the doorway into the kitchen, stopping only to draw a breath.

Allan Holliday said, "Good Lord! What's—" He held out his arms and she flung herself against him with enough force to almost knock him backwards.

"A rat! It ran across my foot! I felt its little claws on me! Then I heard something in the laundry room."

"I was on my way down to put some more coal in the furnace," he said. "My Lord, when I heard you scream I thought all the furies of hell were after you."

"Well, rats aren't my favorite animals! And there was somebody in the laundry room, I tell you. I *heard* them!"

Leslie drew away, provoked with herself for breaking down and going to pieces like a silly high school girl. "Well, maybe it was a mouse, or one of those horrid water-bugs that lurk in basements, but I don't care for them greatly either. But it was the scraping sound that came from the laundry room that really got to me."

He looked at her from the open doorway. "Why did you happen to go down to the basement in the first place? And without a flashlight!"

"Because I wanted to make some coffee, dammit! And I was afraid to try to use that butane thing David brought over." She looked out the kitchen window and saw great plumes of white rising high in the sky over by the place where the Thurston Overstock house had once stood. The thermometer outside the window registered fifteen below zero. "And I didn't think about the flashlight until I was halfway down. See, I didn't even know the lights went out last night because when I went to bed they were still on."

"That's right, they were. You went up and turned on the electric blankets for all of us. Look, Leslie, I dropped the flashlight in the dining room when I was coming through," he said. "That's probably the scraping sound you heard, magnified by the hardwood floor where it rolled off the rug. But I wouldn't be surprised if a rodent had come in from the cold. This time of year, they'll get inside a house even if they have to gnaw their way through concrete. Are you all right?"

Leslie gave him a crooked grin. "Sure. I'm fine. I'm just sorry I screamed loud enough to scare you —and probably wake Aunt Rose. Maybe even the Hansons, and anyone else within a mile of the house."

But Leslie wasn't convinced it was the sound of the flashlight rolling across the floor that she'd heard. There'd been more of a scratching noise, not a sound of an object rolling; and the dining room was to the left of the basement staircase, not the right, where she'd heard the noise. But she wasn't going to argue. Instead, she was going to go upstairs and get into some clothes, then maybe tunnel her way across to the cottage to make sure the Hansons were all right. The cottage was equipped with a wood-burning stove, one of the newer models that had recently come on the market since the energy crunch, and Rose had installed it because of the frequent power outages. One thing she wasn't going to do was go back to that basement, not even if the lights came on. "Can you make coffee in a pan?" she asked.

"Sure. Drop in the coffee after the water comes to a full, rolling boil, then take it off the fire."

She handed him the canister of coffee. "Okay, I put eight cups of water in the pan and the coffee measurer is inside the canister. I'm going to run over to the cottage. I think I'll tell Mrs. Hanson to stay home until the lights come on, though. They keep a supply of food in the house and they can cook on the top of their Fisher stove. Oh—I was going to change clothes first, but my robe is already wet from when I fed the birds, so I'll just wait until I get back and then get into dry clothes."

Rose awakened much earlier than was her custom, but she continued to lie in bed and try to concentrate on plot and dialogue for her book because she'd dropped off to sleep before she had it all in place. She knew there was absolutely no use in sitting down to the typewriter until she decided what to do with the young female protagonist who seemed to be falling in love with the wrong man. But her thoughts skittered off in the direction of Allan

Holliday, the interesting and very attractive man who had blown into her life along with the blizzard. He was so easy to talk with. So pleasant. Yet he appeared not to make any kind of effort to be pleasant—men who were obviously trying to be charming really turned her off. Allan was— Oh, Lord, she thought as she turned over again, I've got to get Wendy straightened out, make her realize that she's only infatuated with this guy Derek, and —let's see—oh, yes, I've got to work out the chase scene with John becoming involved. Hmmmm. Back in Chapter Three I deliberately mentioned the abandoned rock quarry northwest of town and— ummm—yes, John Dillard will ride out there, umm-hmmm—

A shrill scream rose from somewhere below, and even though the bedroom door was closed she had heard the dropped flashlight (although she had no idea what in the world had caused the noise), then the pounding footsteps in the basement stairway, then Leslie's babble followed by Allan's deep, reassuring voice. She was out of her bed like a streak of light and down the steps in seconds, barefoot, throwing her robe around herself along the way.

Her heart pounding as she raced toward the kitchen, Rose heard Leslie say something about cooking on a Fisher stove and then the back door closed. "Allan!" she shouted.

"Everything's all right, Rose. Leslie was frightened by something, probably a mouse, that ran across her foot when she was starting up the stairs."

"What in the world was she doing in the basement, Allan?"

"She wanted to make some coffee. She didn't

know the lights were off, of course, and found out the coffee maker wouldn't work, so she took a pan of water down to the basement to heat it on top of the furnace. Well, it's dark down there, you know, because of all the snow piled up above the windows, and something scurried across her foot and scared the daylights out of her. She's all right. She's gone over to check on the Hansons.''

Rose drew a trembling breath. "But what about the butane burner David brought over here? I guess she didn't think about using it.''

Allan's eyes twinkled. "I believe she said she was afraid of the thing. Rose, Leslie isn't the capable person you are, you know. She's terrified of electricity, and I suppose the butane burner seemed like some sort of a death-dealing contraption to her. At any rate, water's going to be hot enough to make coffee in a few moments. I'm going down to check on the coal in the furnace and I'll bring the pan of water up if it's ready to add coffee. Where are your pan lids? I'll need one to keep this camp-style coffee hot.''

Rose opened the door of a cupboard where pan lids were arranged by size and said, "I don't know what pan she used, but one of these will do, I'm sure. I'll run back up and get myself dressed.''

For a moment, Rose stood there considering the awful fact that it could have been Allan Holliday who had done something to cause her niece to scream. She couldn't imagine what, but there was that possibility that had to be faced, much as she disliked the prospect because she had found herself liking this man more and more all the time. Perhaps he'd just glossed over an action of his own by saying

Leslie was frightened by a little mouse. Her stomach churned. She certainly did not want to blurt out an accusation, but yet—

"Rose, you're trembling! What's the matter?" He quickly covered the few steps between them and put a hand on her arm. "Leslie's all right, I tell you. She's gone over to check on the Hansons to make sure everything's okay there."

Rose bit her lower lip. Finally she looked at him and said, "What else happened, Allan?"

He laughed. "Oh, she thought she heard someone in the laundry room but I'm sure it was just the noise of the flashlight I dropped when I came through the dining room. Leslie's a bit high-strung, I'd say."

The first thought that crossed her mind had to do with Allan's explanation of the noise she had heard —the flashlight falling to the floor had been the cause of it. The second thing she was conscious of was that as far as she was concerned, it was all right for someone in the family to mention one of them was high strung, but definitely not all right for an outsider to say it. But hiding her annoyance, Rose decided she'd go back upstairs and dress as she'd said, and if Leslie wasn't back in just a few minutes she'd run over to the cottage herself. All the while she was dressing she kept thinking about Holliday's comment and realized there was a strange side of Leslie she'd never known until the girl called off her wedding so suddenly.

It was when she was putting on her knee hose that the insidious thought struck her. Could it be possible that Leslie was in back of the "haunting of Overstock House?" How awful! Even to think of such a thing! But still, how well did she really know

116

her niece? How well does anybody ever know anyone? And Leslie had recently undergone a shattering experience; perhaps it had left her more than just high strung. Rose well remembered the day Irene had called to say Leslie was coming to Nevada to see if she could find work in one of the Government offices.

"She's had a terribly traumatic experience, Rose. I think it's a good idea for her to get away from home for a while."

"But what happened? I was getting ready to come to the wedding!"

"There won't be any wedding! Leslie has called the whole thing off, and won't say why. Just said it would never work."

"Oh, dear!" Rose had been overwhelmed with sympathy for Leslie.

"So there we were," Irene had continued, "with the bridesmaids' dresses all finished, and Leslie's wedding gown in the process of having the sleeves put in, and the cake ordered, and the photographer engaged, and all the flowers—Leslie was going to carry roses in the center of her bridal bouquet, you know—well, out of the blue she just came into my bedroom and told me the wedding was off. She wasn't hysterical or anything, Rose, just coldly and matter-of-factly said the wedding was *off*. Well, I'll not pry. I'm sure she'll tell me about it in her own time."

"Yes, of course, it would be better that way. Leslie's never been a giddy person, one to jump madly from one thing to another. She must have had a good reason."

During the short time the girl had been living with her, Rose had never mentioned the wedding that didn't take place. She had thoughtfully taken back to the department store in Reno the wedding gift she had selected and had presented Leslie with a lovely pair of emerald earrings instead. "I saw these in a window, Leslie," she'd said, "and thought how becoming they'd be with your hair worn the way you usually do and your flawless complexion."

Everything had seemed to be fine. Leslie had settled in and seemed to enjoy her work and had met several young people at church and at the Little Theatre group in Virginia City where Rose served on the board of directors, and she'd dated David Dedrick now and then, and had gone out with other young men with whom she worked. It was revolting for her to even consider such a thing, but Rose wondered if, underneath it all, the experience had somehow deranged her niece's mind, and all the apparent normalcy was just a facade.

Telling herself that it was nothing but her over-worked imagination, that she should confine her flights into fantasy to her books, Rose hurried into blue slacks and a velvet top of matching blue, stepped into casual shoes and flew back down the stairs. What rubbish she had allowed herself to think. She herself would have been frightened if a mouse had crawled across her foot in the dark, and had heard an ear-shattering noise over her head! A cup of coffee would put everything into perspective, she was sure, even if the coffee had been made on top of the furnace.

And Allan, of course, had done nothing to cause Leslie to cut loose with that scream. He was, in the first place, a kind man—otherwise he would not have been in the house at all. He could just as easily as not have left Leslie in the parking lot with an inoperative car, tooled off into the night, and spent the evening in the company of some State people in Carson City or with some beautiful woman, or, for all she knew, fed quarters or dollars into the slot machines. He could just as easily have ignored a girl in distress and driven away to develop his day's accumulation of photographs, made plans for several more profitable days doing the job that had given him all that coverage she'd found about his work in Atlanta, instead of spending time checking out wiring, shoveling snow, searching an old house from top to bottom for some evidence of an individual who was perpetrating a hoax.

Allan poured more coffee for her, and Rose glanced at her watch. Leslie had been gone seven minutes, and she gave her two more minutes before she intended to grab a coat and tear out the back door toward the Hansons'. Even though she had come to the conclusion that Allan could not have been telling anything but the truth, she was still concerned about Leslie. Those drifts could be treacherous, she knew, and there was the possibility that Leslie had fallen, even now lay face down in the snow and freezing to death.

The sound of laughter brought an end to her worries. Leslie was coming up the walk that connected the cottage with the back door, giggling as she lifted her feet high then plunked them down in the deeply indented steps she had made on the trip the first time. Her face was flushed, her eyes bright, as she burst into the warm kitchen, bringing the scent of wood smoke and outdoors with her along with a blast of cold air. "They're both all right. Mrs.

119

Hanson made me drink a cup of coffee before I came back. Gee, it was good! And how are you two enjoying the furnace-top brew?"

"Better than nothing, love," said Rose.

"Better than instant, anyway," said Holliday. "You know, I've never believed that a real coffee drinker could put up with the instant product unless he or she were lazy as sin."

Rose laughed. "Perhaps you noticed my coffee maker was set up to brew the maximum quantity. I was just thinking—I'll bet Mitch LeBlanc is up here before long. He'll not wait for the county men, he'll plow off the road between his place and the Dedricks, at least. The county people do get here eventually, Allan, in spite of what Mitch says. He just doesn't want to wait—and besides, I think he enjoys complaining about it."

"Shall we shovel off the driveway before Mitch gets here, Leslie, or shall we wait until he's gone past?"

Rose spoke before Leslie could reply. "I think you'd better wait. I'm at a point in my book where I need the opinion of a person much younger than myself, Leslie. Would you come upstairs with me so I can decide which way to go with my plot?"

For a moment Leslie was puzzled. Rose had never before asked an opinion of her in regard to one of her books. She was able to throw herself into a character so thoroughly that she could think his or her thoughts, use the correct body language, know instinctively how the person would react to whatever came along, whether that character be young or old. Leslie's eyes widened slightly and she hesitated for a second, then her intuition took over and she said, "Sure. I'll make up my bed and be right with you."

120

"Will you excuse us, Allan?" Rose turned and touched his hand.

"Certainly. I'll put a proper pot of coffee on David Dedrick's butane burner and see if there's something on the radio he brought over that might give us a clue about the weather. I'd really like to get back to Reno as soon as the road's open. For one thing, I need a change of clothes pretty desperately. I'm beginning to look—and probably smell—like one of the great unwashed."

Color rose in her cheeks as Rose laughed self consciously and said, "I could launder your clothes while you went back to bed, but until the electricity comes on there won't be any water available."

"Of course. The pump needs electricity in order to function. And I brushed my teeth and washed my hands without thinking!"

"Oh, Lord. I drew water for the coffee, too!" Leslie said.

"Nothing to worry about, I'm sure. There's usually enough in the reserve system to brush teeth and flush the john a time or two, but we'll have to remember not to use any more. I'm glad you found the extra toothbrush, Allan. I always keep one in the guest room."

Holliday said he'd get some buckets and bring in snow to melt for emergency use. "But not to drink, I'm afraid. There's too much junk floating around in the air for melted snow to be safe for drinking, and there isn't anything to use for an improvised filtering system, is there?"

"No, there isn't," Rose replied. "But if you want to make some coffee on the butane stove, there's an old perc pot in the pantry, and you can use the water in the teakettle. It's always kept full. And there's a supply of bottled water in the pantry, too. I always keep two or three gallons on hand. I really prefer to use it for iced tea. Okay, Leslie, I'll be ready for you in a few minutes."

Allan Holliday was looking for the percolator when Rose and Leslie left the room. By the time they reached the staircase they heard him say triumphantly, "Aha! Here it is!" and begin whistling *Stout-Hearted Men* as he measured out coffee and poured water from the kettle into the pot. Leslie giggled. "He seems to know his way around a kitchen, doesn't he!"

"Indeed he does, dear. I wouldn't give a hoot in hell for a man who has to depend on a woman to do the most elementary things for him. Now Leslie, don't go ringing wedding bells," Rose admonished in a whisper, "I merely agree that Allan is a very pleasant person, and nothing more."

They had come to the landing at the top of the stairs, and Leslie whispered, "Is that what you wanted to talk to me about, Aunt Rose? I picked up on the idea that the book was a cover-up."

"Oh, no, of course not. It's about—" Rose paused and listened, wanting to make sure she was not overheard. Holliday's whistled melody changed to *dum, dee-dee-dum, dee-dee-duh, dee-dee-duh* and she went on, "I ran across something last night that might point to the identity of the person who is trying to scare me out of my house. Hurry!"

VIII

After she'd made sure the door was closed behind Leslie, rose said without preamble, "Veronica LeBlanc."

"Oh, Aunt Rose! We agreed Veronica could not possibly be in back of this. With her disability and all—"

"I know. But last night while I was trying to get myself in the mood for sleep, I read through everything I could find about the descendants of Peter Overstock, or anyone even vaguely connected with the family, for that matter, and came across something that just might be the tie-in we've been looking for."

"But I don't see how—"

"Listen, dear. It didn't make too much of an impression when I read it last night, but then I recalled Mitch having said he met Veronica in Yuma. She was also a member of the Church of Latter Day Saints. Okay. Supposing there was an illegitimate child born to Thurston and Becky Overstock. Even though there's never been a shred of gossip to the effect that there *was* a child, how do we know there was not? There was gossip that Thurston visited Becky on occasion. And everyone knows it was Thurston who acted as Becky's friend in court when Peter had been so cruel to her. Well, I've figured out that if there were a child, it was probably placed for adoption, simply because that would have been the best way to hush it up. The geneaology of the Jacobsen family that was in that book I've had for a while but just now got around to reading goes back to 1883 with the mention of a Veronica O. Ledford, born in 1867, who married Arnold Jacobsen. They were the parents of a daughter, Livonia, born in 1885. Livonia married a Sherman Fielding in 1910. They were parents of a daughter called Livonia Veronica, born in 1914. Livonia married an Archibald Jacobsen, a distant relative, in 1930, and now— if Veronica LeBlanc's father's name was Archibald —everything fits."

"Almost everything," Leslie admitted. "But we don't know for sure that the first girl was adopted. You're just assuming that because her middle initial was an 'O', which could have been for Overstock, or could have been a family name like Oswald or O'Brien, or a middle name like Olive or Opal. You've nothing official to go on."

"Court records, dear. I'm pretty sure marriage records are available for 1883, and they should show something. And this is where you come in, Leslie. It would be much easier for you to find out what Veronica's father's name was than it would for me. I've never heard her mention it."

"I get it. You want me to go down and see how

124

Veronica is, since we haven't seen anything of Mitch today."

"Yes. You'll think of how you can bring up the subject. You see, it came to me this morning when I happened to say something to Allan about it being almost time for Mitch to start out with his snow plow, tht Mitch had referred to his mother-in-law as 'Ma Vonnie,' and that was the name of Archibald Jacobsen's wife. Livonia, that is. There's just too many coincidences, Leslie. If Veronica has become interested in genealogy since she's been housebound —and a tremendous number of people are doing their family trees, these days, handicapped or not— and has found out she's a descendant of Becky Over-stock, or even believes she *could* have been, it would provide a motive, don't you see."

"I see, but I still don't see how she could do this number on us."

"Mitch, darling! *He's in on it*, because Veronica isn't able to get out and do the rotten stuff herself, but Mitch is willing to do it because of the money. Veronica's figured out she is a rightful heir, but because of her ancestor's being an illegitimate child, she would probably have a difficult time proving she's a legal heir. So she's got Mitch to do the haunting act, supposing I'll be frightened enough to give up and put the house on the market for a song. Then Mitch and Veronica will grab it up. No one else would want to buy a haunted house, of course, so it would naturally go cheap. And Mitch, that low-down conniver, he's been putting on a big act all the while, trying to make me think he's trying to get next to me. I'd never in this world have thought of Mitch LeBlanc as an actor! Maybe the whole thing is a big act. Maybe Veronica is pretending an illness that doesn't exist and Dr. Kellerman is simply treating her for a mental fixation. Maybe they moved here in the first place because they had it all planned out to wait until some sucker came along and restored the Overstock house, then pretend to haunt the place and drive them out."

"Uh, Aunt Rose . . . I think you've let yourself get carried away! Where did you find all this Jacobsen stuff, anyway?"

"In a little book Dr. Kellerman gave me. It was printed in Reno. Anyone could lay hands on a copy, I'm sure."

"Well, I think you're barking up the wrong tree, but I'll run down and see how Veronica is and what I can find out."

Rose straightened up a few things in her bedroom while there was still plenty of light and then went to the library where she stood for a minute and looked balefully at the electric typewriter. Then she began to check her facts on the abandoned rock quarry so everything would be in readiness for that chapter in the book she was working on, when electric power was restored.

Allan and Leslie hurried out to shovel off the driveway again, and when Holliday said he thought Leslie should stop, she agreed that she was pretty tired. She said that after she warmed up a bit, she'd run down to inquire if Veronica was not feeling well since they'd not seen any sign of Mitch LeBlanc.

"Good enough," said Holliday. "I've got a date with the furnace in about fifteen minutes. Then I think I'll get the snow off the Blazer and hope it'll start."

Leslie returned a half hour later to find her aunt and Allan Holliday enjoying a cup of coffee in the kitchen. Rose Winters gave her an inquiring look, and Leslie returned it with the barest suggestion of a shrug.

"Veronica's all right," she said. "Mitch is, as Veronica says, 'a little poorly today.' "

Rose's eyes said, *Don't keep me in suspense, Leslie!* but she merely asked, "What's the matter with Mitch?"

"Migrane headache. We talked about migraines for a bit, because my mother used to have them, and Veronica said her mother did, too, all her life. Got it from the Wheeler side of the family, she supposed, because her Grandma Wheeler was subject to them, too. I asked her if that was her father's mother, and she said no, reminded me her father was a Jacobsen. It was her mother's mother, Winifred Steinheggen Wheeler. Then she told me all about the Wheelers who came to Yuma several generations back, from a little town in Ohio. I told her we were just concerned about her and hoped Mitch would soon be over his horrible headache and that I would have to be running along. Hated to leave her, really, because Veronica wanted to talk, but I said I thought it best to keep things quiet for Mitch. You remember how Mother always suffered, Aunt Rose?"

"Yes, I do. Couldn't even stand for a curtain to blow in the breeze. And I was younger and couldn't keep still and Mother blistered me more than once for not being quiet when Irene was ill."

"Oh, something else, Aunt Rose. Veronica told me she and Mitch were thinking of leaving Virginia

City. Can you imagine that?"

"No, really? Why, where on earth are they going?"

"You'll miss dear Mitch, Rose," said Allan, teasing her.

"That wretch! No I won't, either. Where are they going?"

"Back to Ohio. Seems one of the Steinheggen relatives left a house and a small farm to Veronica. The Steinheggens had a little money and were really put out when Winifred's daughter, Fanny, married *Anselm* Jacobsen, just over from the old country and trying to make a living as a freight handler. I asked her if her father was related to the well-known Jacobsen clan from around Virginia City, and she said 'None whatever. Jacobsen is a pretty common name in Scandinavia.' "

IX

Morning sun poked insistent fingers at Rose's eyes
and she stirred, blinked and shuddered. Her own
bedroom faced the west. Rose didn't like the early
morning sun, even when it wasn't as dazzlingly
bright as it was right then. She stretched, turned
over and tried to reach into the fuzzy recesses of her
mind for an explanation as to what she was doing in
a bedroom where the sun was breaking into her
sleep. Then it all came back. Leslie had asked her to
share her room, because there were twin beds there,
and she didn't want to sleep alone but preferred a
bed to the sofa in her aunt's room. If there were mice
in the basement, they could quite easily run up the
stairs, and besides, if that unearthly voice disturbed
her sleep again she wanted someone to be with her.

As she left the bed and started toward the window
to see whether it had begun to snow again, Rose recalled how heart-wrenchingly beautiful Leslie had
looked in sleep, those incredibly long lashes sweep-
ing her soft cheeks. Then Rose looked out the

window. For acres, a deep white blanket of snow lay in unblemished splendor. The tips of evergreen trees, their dark green branches laden with pristine white, reached up to a heavenly blue sky. "At least two feet," she breathed, and for a moment lost herself in the sheer beauty spread below. But thoughts of Leslie returned, and she found herself remembering what had been said.

"I'm really all right now, Aunt Rose. It's downright silly of me to not want to spend the night alone. I keep telling myself I'm a big girl and all that. But I'm sure glad Allan Holliday was here when I ran up those basement stairs. He's nice to have around."

"Mmm-hmm. He is, indeed. But now, Leslie—"

Leslie had said the same thing she'd said many times before, but added a new twist:

"You really shouldn't live the rest of your life on memories, Aunt Rose. Uncle Mark wouldn't want that." Then she tossed her brown hair back with both hands and said with calculated guile, "I think Allan Holliday's sending out signals."

Rose felt a tight cold ball in her chest. She put her hand on the outside of it and willed it to go away. It wasn't a physical pain, she knew. She had felt it during the time when Mark had been so sick, when she knew there was no way for the doctors to save him. It had become worse when he had died, when he had been in his casket and she had come home to the empty house in California where she had once known the most exquisite kind of love and contentment. "How do you know your Uncle Mark wouldn't have wanted me to remain alone?" she'd whispered to Leslie. Was it true that people sometimes tended to hold on to their grief, that they became accustomed to the pain of empty living and learned to enjoy it in a sick way? Rose didn't like to think of herself as morbid.

"How do I know Uncle Mark wouldn't want you to go on grieving for him?" Leslie had answered. "I'll tell you. Uncle Mark adored you, but he wanted you to be happy. He talked to me about—well, everyone knows he knew he couldn't get well. He told me he hoped you'd find happiness again, that you'd marry again."

"He didn't say anything like that to me."

"No." Leslie spoke the word slowly. "You see, he knew you weren't exactly receptive to thinking about . . . marrying again, after he died. If you don't believe me, ask Mother. He talked to her about it, too."

Rose listened to the sound of her own heart, beating rapidly. She knew instinctively that the denials she had made the night before about there being a chance of her falling in love with Allan Holliday were due, in part, to her own mixed emotions. Yes, she admitted. She was attracted to the man. Even now, she felt as light-headed as a school girl when she thought about him moving around in her house. Say it, Rose, she admonished herself. Tell the truth. You're infatuated with him and at the same time you feel guilty because you don't want to cast a slur on Mark's memory. She nodded her head and went out into the hall, wondering at the woman thing in her. It seemed a paradox that she was able to manipulate the people she wrote about so well. She knew she wrote with strength and insight. It was easy to understand the motivations of her characters, but when it came to her own life . . . she shrugged.

A pleasant sensation swept over her as she entered her own bedroom. She liked to be with familiar things. Leslie's room was pretty, but it was not *hers*. Looking intently at her reflection in the mirror over the gold and white dresser, she wondered if she had turned into one of those weird characters who could not bear to give up grief. Wallowed in it. Maybe she actually enjoyed being poor dear Rose, such a loving wife, such a terrible blow to have lost her husband to cancer at age thirty-one. The idea appalled her. Started, she looked directly into her blue eyes and found them looking sternly, honestly back at her. She was always a little surprised to see herself in the mirror anyway. It seemed out of keeping to see that unlined face, that golden hair and those dark blue eyes staring back at her when she felt older, sadder, much wiser than she really looked.

"Sick, sick, sick!" she said aloud. Then she felt foolish and was glad to see, through the reflection, something out of place in her room. It was nice to have something to take her mind off herself and the ugly question she had asked of herself. Her lips trembled and finally broke into a wide smile when she realized what Allan Holliday had done. There was the electric coffee pot, plugged into a wall socket, with a cup and saucer on the tray. A single rose blossomed in a bud vase and under the vase was a scrawled note.

"Power is on. I've been in to Carson City where I checked into a hotel. I'm going into Reno to check out the Mapes now that they've cleared the roads. Be back at about eleven, at which time I suggest we go to the library in Reno. We'll have lunch there and

I'd like to take you and Leslie to dinner at the Sharon House tonight.''

Rose lifted the deep pink blossom and noticed it was neither a bud nor was it open all the way. She wondered where in the world he had managed to find a flower shop open so early in the morning.

Breathing in the soft sweetness of the rose, she felt the familiar tightening in her chest. It certainly didn't take Leslie to tell her that Mark was dead. Or to remind her. Her eyes stung with unshed tears as she went into the bathroom to run a quick shower, stopping to pour a cup of coffee on the way. Mark had never brought her coffee in the morning, and he had never left her a rose. But he had done so many other thoughtful things! Her heart cried out in silent protest. It wasn't right to think of someone else the way she was thinking about Allan Holliday. Just two nights ago, she reminded herself, she had suspected Allan was somehow behind the mysterious happenings at the house. She had also begun to wonder about her own niece. It occurred to her that many things can seem sinister when there is no actual foundation on which to build such thoughts.

After she had eaten breakfast, Rose went into the library, took the cover off the typewriter and wrote without a break for two and a half hours. The protagonist in her story had been a mental patient, threatened by the prospect of commitment for the rest of her life. The woman had collapsed after an accident that had caused the death of her fiance. She blamed herself because she had been driving, and there had been an argument. Rose, drawing on her vast research in the area of emotional disturbances, was showing the reader clearly that the young woman actually felt the need to be punished—even if it meant commitment. It was because of the need for punishment that Wendy was finding herself drawn to Derek, a womanizer and a wastrel, who had also run afoul of the law. How easy it was for her to make the reader understand the complexity of logic and irrationality in her character's behavior; yet she couldn't understand her own personality conflict. She stopped for a moment and switched off the typewriter, staring at the black and white sheet of manuscript in the machine. Of course she had no feelings of guilt about Mark's death. But she did have a feeling of guilt when she knew the perfectly normal desires of wanting to live a normal life.

"Yes, but how could I begin to even think about another marriage when I've already had perfection?" she asked herself.

"But it wasn't perfection. You would have been bored to death with a perfect husband," she argued back. "Mark was human, but now that he's dead you've turned him into an angel." How hard it would have been for her to live with an angel!

You just don't want to get hurt again, she thought with cutting clarity.

And she knew she had at last faced the truth. Rose had been the younger sister of an exceptionally beautiful girl. Irene had black hair and dazzling blue eyes, a flawless complexion. Besides, Irene had been brilliant, while Rose had found it hard to concentrate on school work. Irene had been a tough act to follow. Rose had not said it, but her father had. All her life she had felt lost in the shadow of her sister's great beauty, greater intellect. During her school years she had gone to school to the same teachers who had taught Irene. They had been kind; not a one of them had mentioned the joy it had been to have had Irene in their classroom, but Rose had always felt they were thinking it was too bad Irene couldn't have been endowed with just a little less of everything in order that Rose should have something! In her junior year of high school she had fallen madly in love with her chemistry teacher. William Ellison was teaching school for the first time. He had spoken pleasantly to Rose because he was a kind man, but Rose, the shy student, had mistaken his natural interest in her for something else. Then William Ellison had met her sister Irene, and that had been that. Except for unimportant dates, Rose had been the one who stayed at home, read books and daydreamed. She had never had a serious romance in her life until she met Mark Winters. Even with Mark she hadn't been at all sure he wouldn't see Irene, already married to William Ellison, and find the younger sister dull and unlovely.

It had taken her years to be able to even pretend to be sure of herself. If Mark had ever given her the impression that he was inclined to stray, she knew she would have been crushed. He had not. In his very precious way, he had made her into a complete woman, and now she knew the old fears were hovering in the background, waiting to pounce. Doctor Kellerman would have made a good husband, there was no doubt in her mind about that. There had been other men, too, in those years since Mark had died. And in spite of her denial of it to Mitch LeBlanc, Doctor Kellerman *had* asked her to marry him, although he was also the only one who had done so. But Rose was woman enough to realize that it takes a little encouragement for a man to ask the all-important question. She had encouraged nobody, not even the doctor. Because she was neurotic? Like the woman in the story she was writing? Oh, no! That woman was completely different. She had invented a completely different situation. The woman in the book felt she was responsible for the death of her fiance, couldn't she understand that? After all, she had created the character and the plot, established the circumstances, caused the woman to flee from reality.

Because reality was too painful, she had made the reader understand.

The same as . . . the same for her, for Rose, then? Not that reality *was* too painful, but the mere fact that it could become difficult if she strayed from the comfortable role of grieving widow.

What a terrible point of view! She realized it was, but she also was honest enough with herself to realize that it was her point of view. She was not much better off than the woman in her current book. No wonder Leslie was bringing in stray men and every time she called her sister or received a letter from her she was disturbed by what she had felt was an increasing tendency to inquire if there was a man in the picture. Even her mother asked when she was going to start living again.

The Victorian clock on the mantel told her it was almost ten-thirty. Allan had said in his note he would return for her at eleven. There was time for her to make a call to Irene.

Rose's sister sounded much like Leslie. She answered on the second ring, vibrant and very much interested, even before she knew the call was from

Rose. "How's Leslie?" she asked after they had exchanged the amenities.

"Just getting along splendidly," answered Rose. "She loves her job."

"No moping, or anything? About Phillip, I mean?"

"No, as a matter of fact, she isn't. I haven't mentioned anything to her about Phillip and the wedding and all. I felt—well, it would be unpleasant for her."

"And you," said Irene a little tartly. "You dislike anything unpleasant, don't you? Oh, well, I still adore you, Rose. Is Leslie seeing anybody?"

"Yes, she's seeing a lot of a boy named David Dedrick. He's going to the University of Nevada. Political Science. Really, a brilliant young man, but of course I suppose I'm a little old-fashioned. I can't get used to these beards and long hair."

"Beards and long hair are *out*, according to what I read."

"Not in this area, Irene. But David is a nice clean-cut fellow."

"Well, I'm glad she's seeing somebody. How about you? Have you managed to come out of your shell long enough to look about you and see if there are any available men around your age?"

"Ah . . . as a matter of fact, Leslie brought home a man the other night for dinner. He's Allan Holliday. The photographer."

"Oh, really! Now, for a change, will you sort of act a little human?" While Irene was saying that, the doorbell rang. She knew Allan had returned, or at least she supposed that was he ringing the chimes. Hurriedly, she told her sister about the voice and the fright they'd experienced in the night. Over and above the conversation, she could hear the murmur of voices in the house. Mrs. Hanson must have answered the door and Allan was waiting for her.

"You must have been scared out of your wits," Irene was saying sympathetically. There was also a note of alarm in her voice.

"We were. Leslie slept in my room night before last, I slept in hers last night."

"But it must have been comforting to have a man in the house."

"It was, but, well, it sounds silly now, but I was so paranoid that I even began to wonder if Mr. Holliday mght have something to do with it. Or even Leslie. Today it's almost impossible to realize how ridiculous I was."

"Oh, I don't know. I think most anybody would get a little hysterical under the circumstances. But how do you know for sure it *isn't* a ghost?"

"Oh, Irene, come, now! We know there's no such thing as ghosts."

"No we don't."

"But you've always been so practical!"

"Certainly. But how can one be practical in the face of spirits? Or ghosts or haunts or shades of whatever one might be inclined to call them? That is, if you consider it practical to deny the possibility of the existence of anything we can't see. You can't see gravity, for instance."

"But we can feel the power of it."

"My point exactly. In this world, I think it's a highly bone-headed person who denies anything. Great-grandmother McKennely would hang us all for participating in witchcraft if she were to walk into our homes right now and see television, push-button electric ranges, remote controls for opening garage doors, just imagine! Maybe the soul does live on after the change we call death. If it does live on, maybe it has the power to communicate."

"Oh, Irene! Really, I'm sure we'll find some hanky-panky going on that has more to do with money and property than ghosts and haunting. I have to go now, Irene. Mr. Holliday is here."

"Keep in touch, Rose. And tell Leslie to be a good girl and write us, will you?"

After she hung up the phone, Rose hurried out into the living room, again conscious of a quickening of her pulse at the idea of being in the room with Allan Holliday. The extension rang just as she greeted him. Mrs. Hanson must have picked it up in the kitchen, because it stopped ringing immediately.

"Thank you for the coffee. And the rose." She couldn't keep the smile from her face. "Where in the world did you find a florist open so early in the morning?"

"I didn't. A very important lady politician had apparently checked into the hotel where I went to find a room. A dozen roses must have been delivered during the night. There they were, waiting on the desk with the card, and there I was, paying for my room and accepting my key. So when the man at the desk turned his back my hand just reached out and suddenly there was a rose in it." He was grinning delightedly. "The lady believes in sharing the wealth, so of course, I always do everything I can to help."

For some unaccountable reason, Rose felt very young and giddy. Mrs. Hanson came in and asked her to pick up the extension. It was Leslie. Her young voice sounded very strong and clear as she said, "I'm at work. Just thought I'd call and let you know I'm okay."

"Oh, I'm glad you called. Did you have any trouble getting to work?"

"No, Mr. Holliday took me. The roads had all been cleared."

"And is your car in working order?"

"They said it'd be done by this afternoon. You sound sort of excited. How come?"

"Well, uh—Allan has just returned from Reno. We're going to the library right now. Oh, he's invited us to dinner."

"I have a date. Besides, I wouldn't want to be hanging around like a spare tire. Two's company, you know. Thaw out a little, Auntie. Have champagne with your dinner. Got to rush, now!"

"Wait! I just talked with your mother and she isn't discounting the fact that we might have a real ghost on our hands. I think she feels it's more interesting. Sometimes I think she should have been the writer."

"Too lazy. I'll see you later, Aunt Rose."

Later, Rose Winters would remember the youthful ring in her niece's voice when she said she would see her later. It had been such a very normal thing to say.

X

The ride into Reno was beautiful. On both sides of the highway the snow was piled high, bright and dazzling under the sun. As soon as they were seated in the Blazer, Rose asked if they could take the Carson City road. Allan looked at her skeptically. "Are you afraid of my driving?"

"Not your driving. The roads."

"But they've cleaned off the snow."

"I know, but it's freezing. Geiger Grade is so steep and if there's ice, I'm afraid I might go to pieces. I'm terribly afraid of that treacherous stretch of mountains under the best of conditions."

"I'm not arguing with you, but how about Gold Hill? When I took Leslie to work this morning I had a few bad moments myself."

"Well, it's like this: Gold Hill is bad. But when you're over that one, it's relatively flat all the way."

He smiled, and told her she'd better put her sun glasses on. The Blazer was surprisingly comfortable. After they had turned onto U.S. 395, Rose took a deep breath and settled back in her seat. She was wearing a blue suit under her fur coat and when the heater made it uncomfortably warm she shrugged out of the coat. He helped her, making her nervous because she felt he should use both hands for driving. "That's a lovely shade of blue you're wearing. It matches your eyes, exactly."

"Thank you. It's getting so it isn't easy to find clothes suitable for a mature woman. Most clothes seem to be designed for teenagers. Even Leslie has trouble finding things appropriate for office wear."

"You could wear anything," he said with a wicked gleam in his eyes as he glanced at her. "But if I had anything to say in the matter, I'd prefer a skirt slit up the side so you could show off your legs. You have beautiful legs, Rose. What's that bright and shining building there on our left?"

"Oh, that's the Steen mansion. Mr. Steen was one of the first people in the country to make millions of dollars from a uranium mine. He raises beautiful Arabian horses, too."

"I've read about him. I think there've been several articles in national magazines about the Steen millions."

"He's very cordial, I understand. If you wanted to photograph his home, I'm sure he'd be very happy. His wife is a gracious lady, too. And the house is absolutely beautiful."

"Not this trip. Perhaps another time. This time I want to do just the old silver mining mansions. The Bowers place is somewhere close, isn't it?"

"Yes . . . let me see—there's the Club Jubilee. Oh, yes. It's around here somewhere."

"Tell me about the Bowers people."

Great wisps of sparkling mist rose high into the

sky as they passed the hot springs. "Well, there's not too much that can be put in a few words. Eilly ran a boarding house of sorts, and Sandy had a claim to a mine. It's a tragic story, really. Legend has it that when they went to get married they rode on a burro, and Sandy didn't want to wear shoes. She was rather socially ambitious, and of course after they made the famous Comstock strike Eilly thought the world should be at her feet. She had the mansion built and Sandy never felt very comfortable in it. He wasn't a good businessman, either. He turned over a lot of stock to someone who wasn't at all scrupulous and all of Eilly's priceless possessions went to pay back bills. That happened after he died. I think she always wanted a child. She adopted one or two, but they both died. I'm sure it was two children she adopted. They're supposed to be buried over there in back of the house. We're coming up on it now."

He slowed down and looked out the window at the impressive facade. "I understand Mrs. Bowers ended her life in San Francisco, without funds." He sounded morose.

"Some say she told fortunes for a living. She was supposed to have been endowed with second sight. It didn't bring her much happiness, I'm afraid. But yes, she did die in San Francisco."

He parked the car on a side street close to the library. "Let's go in and see if they have anything on your house."

"It's a beautiful library, isn't it?" Rose looked around fondly at the trees that were growing inside, at the mass of potted plants and all the airy spaciousness. "I was thinking about doing a book about a girl who lived in a library, a university

143

student, perhaps. I must think about that again some day."

"You'd have her hiding, I suppose." Allan looked around at the free-standing reading rooms, at the three visible floors of book stacks. "It sounds intriguing. Almost plausible."

"Nevada reference works are over there," she said, indicating a large area.

They read steadily for over an hour when Allan announced he was starving. "Let's have lunch now, and return later."

Not much about the Overstock mining operations turned up during the morning, but in the afternoon Rose looked up from the big book she'd been skimming through and said, "This is interesting." She hitched her chair closer to his and they read together.

"In 1862, the brothers built identical mansions on a site not far from Gold Hill. The houses were built of Bedford limestone, brought from southern Indiana by wagon. Parquet floors of the finest hardwood were in every room, only to be covered by imported Oriental carpets. Fine lace curtains from Belgium decorated the pretentious leaded glass windows. The furnishings, of elaborate Zambezi mahogany and walnut, were brought around the Horn. Each home boasted a concert grand piano, exquisite silverware from France (the silver having been taken from the Becky Anne mine and sent to France where artisans fashioned it into plates and dinnerware). Thurston's home was resplendent with priceless paintings, while Peter preferred to invest in jewels for his beautiful wife."

"Wonder what ever became of the jewels!" Allan murmured. "Do you suppose—"

"That they might be hidden somewhere in the house? Oh, Allan! No. They couldn't be. With all the rennovation that was done, if there were any jewels they'd have turned up long ago."

"Well, it's an idea. But I guess we might as well call it a day."

Out on the street, Rose was surprised to see that it was already dark. The garish neon signs were lighting up downtown Reno. "It's after six," Allan said as they pulled away from the curb. "Would you mind if I stopped by the hotel in Carson City and made a quick change before I take you home? I take it you don't want to go the Geiger Grade way, so we'll be in Carson anyway."

"Sure. Fine. Oh, by the way, Leslie isn't going to dinner with us. She has a date, she said."

"All right. Oh, there's a house I want to see from the outside while I'm here. It'll only take a minute. Do you know where Park Street is? Or Willow?"

"I don't know much about Reno, to tell you the truth," said Rose.

"There's a big Victorian house at the corner of Park and Willow. I saw an artist's sketch of it sometime ago in the school administration building. The house is being used as a guest house for people who come for divorces, mostly, I believe, but there's quite a history connected with it. It used to sit on the site of the Holiday Hotel. Three stories high, it was cut in two pieces and moved several years ago to the present site. If I can find it tonight, I can come and ask the owners if I can photograph it for the series sometime later."

Rose said she didn't mind. She looked at Allan's profile as he flicked on the overhead light and looked

145

intently at the map.

"It isn't far," he said. "Just a few blocks, according to this map."

They drove in silence through the slushy streets. It was always a source of amazement to Rose to realize that Virginia City was so much colder than Reno. There had apparently been very little snow, and what there had been had almost melted by the time they had arrived earlier. She was startled out of her reverie when Allan said, "Hell! It should be here, but it isn't."

"Are you sure you're at—what was it, Park and Willow?" She looked around. A one-story apartment house was on one side of the street, an empty lot on another. Lights shone from the two other corner houses. They bore no resemblance to a Victorian mansion three stories high.

A man came around the corner of the empty lot. He carried a flashlight. Allan rolled down the window and called. "Sir, could you tell me where I might find a big old Victorian house with a lot of gingerbread on it? It was supposed to have been moved from the Holiday Hotel site to the corner of Park and Willow?"

"Oh, that used to be right here," said the man. "They called it the Elmhurst. It burned to the ground. A shame. A real nice old house, too. They say it was arson. I loved right up the street when it happened. A real damned shame."

"How long ago was that?"

"Oh—" The man scratched his chin. The flashlight bobbed up and down, casting the light skywards in a moving arc. "I guess that was five, maybe six years ago. Couldn't say for sure."

"Well, that's that. Thanks."

Rose felt herself shudder. She thought she might have been chilled by the cold air when the window had been open. She also had known a moment's sick feeling when the man had mentioned arson. It was such an ugly word. She wondered about the people who had been living in the house at the time; wondered if they had put as much love and care into the restoration of their house as she had into her own. Later, she wondered if she had not experienced a premonition, because almost immediately, she began to worry about Leslie.

"But what could have happened to her?" asked Allan.

That was the trouble with most men, decided Rose fretfully. They were always so reasonable. It didn't do a thing to dispel her feeling of something sinister hanging over her head, something that pertained to her niece, for Allan to point out the fact that Leslie was a good driver.

"I know, but—"

"But what?"

"I just feel apprehensive. I wish we hadn't stopped to see if we could find that other house. I wish we hadn't stayed at the library so long."

"But we did. You're borrowing trouble."

"Maybe so, but I think we'd better go the shortest possible way."

Allan sounded amused. She could no longer see him clearly, but she could hear his rather exasperated voice that was only faintly tinged with a smile. "What about your unfounded fears of the bad curves and the steep grade?"

"Well, it's dark now. I won't see them, so I won't be as much afraid."

"Pure logic," he said agreeably. "I've always

admired a logical woman." If she hadn't been paying attention to what he was saying, she would never have realized he was being sarcastic in the pleasantest way possible. She was glad he couldn't see that she had her eyes tightly closed when they got to the dizzying incline that went almost straight up to the summit. She knew perfectly well that the sheer drop was right there, and she tried not to think about how it would feel to go hurtling over the edge five-thousand feet below. She opened her eyes a couple of times to see where they were. When she saw the sign that said *Visit the Bucket of Blood*, she knew she had almost made it.

"The house is all dark," she said quietly as they pulled into the driveway.

"Maybe the lights have gone out again."

"But look all around us. Mine is the only house that doesn't have lights."

"I don't understand this, Rose. I've checked the wiring so thoroughly—"

"I don't either, but—" Rose stood stock still, her eyes riveted on the wide open doorway. "The door's wide open!"

Allan took her arm. "Now, don't get excited. The wind has been high. I didn't say anything, but it was difficult to keep the Blazer on the road there a couple of times. It's probably just blown open."

Something just inside the doorway moved. Suddenly Rose felt her knees going weak under her. She gasped and swayed a little. She knew there should at least be a faint glow of candle light, even though the electricity was off. Their footsteps sounded very loud on the porch. "Did you see that— that—whatever it was just inside the door? It moved."

"I didn't see anything." He tightened his grasp on her arm. "Stop shaking, will you?"

Mark would never have sounded so impatient. The thought flittered across her mind as they went through the wide open doorway. A blast of air that felt much colder than the outside met them full in the face.

"Leslie?" Rose called her niece's name, then waited, listening for an answer.

Allan took a flashlight out of his pocket and flicked it on. Papers were blowing about inside the entrance hall. A stiff breeze was blowing through the house. The beam of the light ate a yellow hole into the blackness. "There's got to be another door open to cause this draft."

"Mrs. Hanson!" Rose called the cook's name, knowing full well that nobody was going to answer. The house was silent as a tomb except for the eerie sound of the wind that blew in gusts through the first floor rooms. And carried in the wind was the faraway, yet terrifying close words, whipping along, echoing, plaintive, weak, yet sometimes strong: "Help, Becky. Help me! Becky!"

Yes, there was no doubt about it. Allan was certainly right. Right all the way. Yes indeed. The back door was wide open, the curtains were blowing every which way, and yes! There most assuredly was a draft. The crazy, crisp thoughts fluttered through her mind even though the darkness was getting darker and a roaring that had nothing to do with the cold wind that blew through the house was in her ears. The darkness and the roaring sound were going to drag her right down there. Where? Someplace. Anyplace. She must not, absolutely must not give in to it. The house was gone and

Leslie was empty. No, that wasn't right at all. The house was dark and Leslie was gone. Yes. That was right.

"Rose! Darling!"

She heard Allan's voice and she heard him call her "Darling," but she couldn't fight the thing that wanted to pull her down any longer. It was taking her a long time to fall to the floor. Perhaps he would catch her before she fell all the way.

XI

Bright lights spun around crazily and the coffee pot was making those insane thirp-thirp sounds. "So that's what it feels like to faint," said Rose. She was looking up into Allan's face, thinking she really ought to ask where she was. But she knew where she was. She was in her own kitchen, the doors were closed, the lights were on, and Mrs. Hanson's solid-looking feet and legs were standing there by the stove. She smelled the coffee.

"She always makes the coffee on the stove," she heard herself say for no good reason at all. "She says if God meant for us to have electric coffee pots He'd have put electricity in them, the same as the timer."

"Haven't you got some brandy somewhere?"

"Oh, sure. It's in the liquor cabinet."

"Looks to me like you already had a little something," said Mrs. Hanson's voice disapprovingly.

"No, I didn't. You know very good and well I seldom have a thing to drink . . ." She gasped, sat up, and looked at the odd angle of the kitchen cabinets from her viewpoint on the floor. "Leslie! Where is she? Mrs. Hanson, where is Leslie?"

"I don't know. I swear to God, I don't know. She was right here in the house when the lights went out. I could hear her upstairs, she said she was going to have dinner with that hippie boy, and did I think she ought to wear that new red dress, then she went right on upstairs and there came this gust of wind. It blew open the kitchen door. But I could hear water running. You know that noise it always makes in the pipes when you run water in the blue bathroom. Well, I just took it for granted she was in the tub. Then the lights went out. After that, there was that *thing*. You know—the voice."

"But you said you heard her upstairs." Rose was no longer weak and trembling with fear. She was afraid, but she felt stronger, more able to cope.

"I did. I heard her scream bloody murder."

"Did you go upstairs?"

"Why, of course I went upstairs! Did you think I'd just let her stay up there all by herself in a bathtub, not a light on in the house and ghosts stalking around trying to get in the windows and her screamin' like that?"

"Why did you say that, Mrs. Hanson, about ghosts trying to get in the windows?" Allan's voice was pleasant.

"Because there was this tapping sound on the outside of the house, that's why. All over, it seemed like. Now, that's a new wrinkle. Before, it was just the voice and the cold and those words. I didn't know if she had a candle up there or not, so I lit one and went right up. If you want to know the truth

152

about it, I didn't feel too easy about being down-stairs all by myself anyway."

"*Did* she have a candle?"

Mrs. Hanson shrugged. "I wouldn't know, Mrs. Winters. She wasn't there. She just . . . well, there isn't any other way to say it. That girl just simply *disappeared.*"

"Nobody just disappears," said Rose.

"I know it, but Leslie did, just the same."

"She probably came down the back stairs as you were going up the front ones," Rose insisted.

"If she did, she's walking around outside in this freezing weather, naked as a jaybird. If you'll just give me a chance, I'll tell you. I went up there like I said and knocked on the bathroom door, but Leslie didn't answer. There wasn't a sound coming from her room, either. So after I'd knocked again, I just quicklike opened the door and went into the bathroom. I was standing in the room you gave Mr. Holliday last night. I was just completely dumb-founded when I didn't see her. What was worse, there was her robe, hanging on the hook on the bath-room door. Every towel right in place, a wet wash-cloth in the bathtub along with a bar of soap and the water still hot. Then in her room I saw her things all laid out on the bed. The red dress, those boots on the floor, her pantyhose and bra and half slip. And there was a purse with fringe on it, too, right there on the bed, a new one, by the looks of it. The old one—that plaid thing she usually carries to work—it was right there by it, and I have an idea she meant to take things out of one purse and put them into another. But something happened to scare her away. Or *take* her away," Mrs. Hanson added as a dark afterthought. "I went all through the house looking for her, but she just wasn't anywhere. I even looked out the window. Then I went all around on the outside of the house and there's not a footprint or anything. She just plain disappeared, I tell you."

Allan Holliday took Rose by the hand. "I'm sure she just threw on something else and left the house. In her fright, she probably didn't think about the clothes she had ready to wear. She undoubtedly forgot about the bathrobe she had taken into the bathroom with her, too. Remember, she has had some pretty bad frights recently." He broke off, glanced at the cook, and she he thought it would be a good idea to go up to Leslie's room so Rose could check through her clothing. "I'm sure you'll find she just slipped into a coat and left the house."

"If you don't need me any more, Mrs. Winters, I'll just go on over to the cottage. I hear my husband right now, at the door."

Footsteps rang against the icy sidewalk and Jim Hanson's soft voice called out. "You in there, Mary? You see anything of the girl yet? I looked all over, but I didn't see hide nor hair of her. Her car's right there in the garage where she—well, hello, Mrs. Winters. I saw the truck out in the driveway, but I just—"

"She isn't in the house, Jim." Mrs. Hanson seemed on the verge of tears.

"We'll find her, Jim," said Rose with a conviction she didn't feel.

"I certainly hope so, Mrs. Winters. I've been trying to call the boy's house, that Dedrick fellow's, for the last few minutes, off and on, but the line's busy. What I kept telling Mary was that the girl just got scared and the boy happened to come right then to take her out, so she ran down the steps the back way just as Mary ran up the front way. You want I should keep on tryin' that number?''

"No, that's all right, Jim. I'll keep trying it."

Mrs. Hanson put on a heavy black coat and a woolen scarf and stuck her hands in her pockets. "Now, I tell you, I won't rest at all until that child is found. I just hope you'll let me know if you find her. She was such a sweet thing, too . . . not a bit like a lot of these young girls that just say the awfullest words imaginable and right out loud and in mixed company, too.''

"I wish she hadn't said, '*Was* such a sweet young thing,' " said Rose after the door had closed.

"Easy," said Allan. The candles spluttered when the door opened and closed behind the Hansons, but they didn't go out. "Just try to take it easy." They started up the front steps together. The flames burned brightly, illuminating the stairway. Once, Rose looked over her shoulder into the pitch dark at the bottom of the stairs. She wished she hadn't. Although she immediately knew those grotesque shapes in back of them were nothing but shadows cast by the light they carried, the movements startled her. Just as they got to the top of the stairs, the lights came on again. The upstairs hallway was plunged into brightness. Leslie's door stood wide open. Allan blew out the candles and tweaked the tips with his fingers to keep them from smoking. They both looked at the bed. Just as Mrs. Hanson had said, Leslie's clothing was lying there. There was the red dress, the new purse, the one the girl had been carrying, the tissue paper stuffing, pantyhose, half slip and bra.

In the bathroom was the long warm robe, hanging

on the hook on the door. Underthings were scattered helter-skelter on the floor, apparently where Leslie had taken off her clothes before stepping into the tub.

"She never left anything lying around," said Rose. She looked at the bathtub. Water was still in the tub. She smelled the lemon scented bath oil her niece used and stuck a hand in to test the water. It was still warm. A bar of soap had fallen to the floor and skittered across the room.

"Do you think you can go through her clothes to see what is missing?" Allan's voice startled Rose, even though he was at her side. She had been looking at the bar of soap, thinking of how terrified Leslie must have felt, how vulnerable.

"I think so."

"Are you afraid to stay upstairs by yourself?"

"No. Not as long as the lights stay on."

"Then I'll go down and try to call the Dedrick boy. Do you know his number?"

Rose supplied the telephone number and went back into Leslie's room where she began a methodical search through Leslie's clothes. Even though the lights were on, she kept the candle close at hand along with a pack of matches. A pleasant fragrance rushed out at her as she riffled through the neatly arranged dresses, pants suits, skirts and blouses. Leslie was organized; belts were carefully arranged on hangers with the matching outfits, all the pants were hung together, all the skirts were together and the dresses were zipped, fastened at the neck and properly hung. There was the pink coat with the fluffy fur collar, the tweed one, the car coat, the camel's hair and the raincoat. A short pink flannel bathrobe was hung over a matching nightgown. A yellow one, almost identical, hung at its side. Shoes were placed side by side on the tiered shelving on the floor, each with shoe trees. Three pairs of boots, one badly scuffed, marched neatly along the back wall. There was a pair of rubber overshoes just inside the door, slightly damp. Leslie had worn them to work that morning. A pair of white velvet bedroom slippers were on the floor in the bedroom. They looked as if she had just stepped out of them. The things Leslie had taken off the other twin bed had been put away. She remembered how quickly the girl had removed the things from the other twin bed the night before. They had been there because Leslie had been sorting through things, getting some ready for the cleaners and others for mending.

Since everything was as neat and orderly as if the girl had just finished arranging her clothing, Rose could only come to the conclusion that either Leslie had something to wear that she had not noticed, or that she was not wearing anything. She put an ice cold hand to her hot face. It was impossible to think of Leslie in that context. She would never *willingly* run around naked. Besides, it was bitter cold outside, and getting colder.

One small ray of hope was left. Maybe the child had gone into her bedroom. If she had been afraid— if someone had been in the house, had come into the bathroom when she was in the tub—she could have run into her aunt's room, locked herself in . . . but no. Mrs. Hanson had said she searched the entire house. Just the same, Leslie could have gone to her room, thrown on something that belonged to Rose, hoping to elude whoever had been after her.

Quickly, Rose went through her own wardrobe.

Nothing was missing.

Allan called from the hall. "The telephone isn't working. I went over to the cottage and used the one there. The Dedrick boy had just left the house. His sister said he should be here within a few minutes. Are any of Leslie's clothes missing?"

"No." Rose felt a small nerve in her left eyelid begin to jump. Her voice was shrill when she said, "Allan, I'd been hoping against hope that David came early, that Leslie was with him! And now—" She put both hands to her face. His arms went around her and he held her tightly.

"I think we'd better call the police."

"And I'll have to call Irene," said Rose. "Oh, this is terrible! Just terrible! Her mother will be frantic!"

"Wait a little while before you call your sister, Rose. We must not panic." He put a hand under her chin and looked deeply into her eyes. "There could still be a perfectly reasonable explanation for her absence."

"Oh, sure." She said it bitterly, but she felt a little better. Allan was there with her. She was not alone.

"Listen, Rose. I may have found something," Allan said. "There are footsteps in the snow. They're all around the side of the house. Of course Jim Hanson could have made them. But, the footprints were very big; I'd say whoever wore those boots would have been an enormous man—maybe a size thirteen shoe—and Mr. Hanson isn't big. I noticed his feet. They seem quite small."

"Yes. Besides, Jim Hanson would not have—. As soon as David gets here I'll call the police."

Allan held her coat for her. "Let's go outside

together, and I'll try to trace the telephone lines to see where they might be down.''

They didn't have to trace very far. Just outside the extention in the library where Rose did her writing the wires had been cut.

XII

David Dedrick's face was ruddy from exposure to the cold. He stood just inside the front door and said he'd wait right there because of his snowy boots. He asked if Leslie would be long.

"Take them off, David," Allan's voice was cordial, but subdued. "I'm afraid we have bad news. Leslie isn't here."

"Not here?" The young man's eyes went from Allan Holliday to Rose. "What do you mean she isn't here? What bad news?"

"Leslie seems to have disappeared, David."

"You're putting me on."

Rose shook her head sadly. As she told him what little they knew, the ruddy cast drained from David's face, leaving it ashen. He slumped to the hall chair and began to take off his boots. "Somebody's killed her. I feel sure of it. Or somebody's going to kill her. My God! Have you called the police?"

"Not yet. We were waiting for you. We had hoped

you'd be able to shed some light on her whereabouts. We tried to call you earlier. As a matter of fact, Mr. Hanson has been trying for quite some time but he said your line was busy." Allan moved toward Rose.

"It was. My sister was talking long distance to her boy friend. For over an hour."

"Then when we finally did get your house, you had just left," said Rose. "Come into the living room. We'll have some coffee."

"I think we should call the police first." The boy headed straight for the telephone.

"The lines have been cut, David," said Allan. "We'll call from the cottage where the cook and her husband live. I'll do it, now that you're here to stay with Mrs. Winters. I didn't like to leave her alone in the house." He picked up the flashlight.

David wouldn't sit down. He kept pacing back and forth across the room. Rose kept getting up and going to the window, hoping without much real hope that she would see Leslie walking toward the house from the road.

"I talked to her earlier. She said she'd found out something about this house, or about somebody, that made her fear for her life. Well, you know how girls sometimes let their imaginations run away with them. I'm afraid I sort of made fun of her. I mean, I thought she was just being dramatic. She got kind of mad at me, and then I asked her to tell me what she meant. We were talking on the phone. This was before she left her office in Carson City. She called me at home. She didn't sound like she was still angry, but she wouldn't tell me. I told her if it was all that important, I mean if it made her feel like her life was in danger, she should let me know. She

161

just sort of laughed and said she'd tell me tonight when we went to dinner."

"She didn't give you any kind of hint?"

"No. I could kick myself for making fun of her. I think she might have said more about it if I hadn't been so skeptical. I said something about the ghost of Overstock House and reminded her that ghosts don't do physical damage."

The scene was so unreal. There she was, going to the window every second to look out into the dark, and there was David Dedrick, pacing up and down in her living room, talking about something neither of them believed in, and there was Allan, calling the police on the Hansons' telephone because Leslie had disappeared into thin air. There was no way to describe the terror that gripped her when she allowed her imagination to dwell on any of the hundreds of things that came into her mind.

Allan came back. "Someone from the Sheriff's department will be here soon. I think we should get everything clear in our minds. Mr. and Mrs. Hanson will be here in a few minutes. I asked them to come over because it was Mrs. Hanson who was here when Leslie disappeared. Rose, if you'd fix some coffee and a sandwich or something, I think we'd be wise to eat a bite. We'd planned to go out to dinner and so had David and Leslie. It's easier to carry on under stress if we are fortified with food."

"I can't think about eating," said Rose. "But I'll fix something for you and David."

"I don't want anything either," David said. "My stomach feels as though I've swallowed a bunch of butterflies."

"Coffee and some juice, then," said Allan. "Anything at all. Just fix something, Rose."

When she was in the kitchen, she had an idea Allan was more interested in getting her out of the room than he was in having her prepare some food. Feeling somewhat ridiculous, she took off her shoes and crept back to the doorway that led into the living room where she listened to David and Allan. David was saying he understood. *Understood what?*

Slowly, Rose realized that Allan had asked David to call his sister and ask her to come and spend the night. "There are twin beds in Leslie's room," Allan was saying. "Rose is concerned about what people say. Although she hasn't said anything about it, I'm sure she would feel her reputation would be damaged if she spent a night alone in her house with me, even under these circumstances. And of course I have no intention of leaving her in this house all alone."

"I'll stay too," said David. "And while she's in the kitchen I'll go over to the Hansons' house and call Lou Ann. But before I go, I want you to tell me what you really think."

"Okay. After the first night I was here—when I brought Leslie home when her car wouldn't start and then I couldn't get back to town—I checked everything thoroughly and didn't find anything out of order as far as the electrical wiring is concerned. Everything in the fuse box seems to be in good shape and I couldn't find anything else that looked out of line. I think someone wants this house, David. I don't believe in the ability of spirits to come back to the land of the living and make themselves known. I think somebody is pretending to be the ghost of Peter Overstock. Anybody could go to the public library and look up the information about the way he met his death. I read the whole story while

Rose and I were there today. No doubt Peter Overstock did call his wife when he was losing his life in the icy waters of Washoe Lake, but I don't believe he would come back here after all these years of being dead and call his wife. I think somebody is trying to make Rose Winters believe the house is haunted. I don't know how much money she invested in the restoration, but work of this kind doesn't come cheap. I think if we can delve into the possibility of a pretend-ghost, we might be able to find out where Leslie is."

"You've discussed this with Rose?"

"Yes. But she can't imagine who it could be. I'm afraid it has to be someone she knows and trusts."

"Why? I don't understand that. Why couldn't it just be someone who has always wanted the house? People get all kinds of fixations. It could be anybody from around here."

"I think it's someone she knows and trusts, because I believe she has allowed the person to come into the house. I've checked this place out pretty thoroughly. I haven't found a secret passageway or a trap door, and I believe I would have if there are any."

"Do you have anybody specific in mind?"

"Yes. Mrs. Hanson. The cook. I might be absolutely wrong, and I hope I am, but did you notice the size of that woman's feet? And if you put a pair of overshoes on over those big feet of hers, you'll have something huge."

"But Leslie told me Mrs. Hanson was afraid of the —she's heard that creepy voice before, and has been scared half out of her mind."

"That could have been an act," said Allan. "She could have manufactured the entire production. Or she could have an accomplice. Her husband, perhaps. I'm not forgetting that we have only Mrs. Hanson's word for it that Leslie disappeared into thin air. According to her story, the two of them were alone in the house."

"Well, I don't know," said David. He sounded unconvinced. "I think they've lived around here for quite some time. My dad would know. He's a history buff, too. He might know if there's a possibility of some connection between the Hansons and this house. He'll be home this weekend and we can ask him. But the whole thing sounds pretty far-fetched to me."

"There are other people around here who would know quite a bit of lore pertaining to the house itself. I think we should go at it from the angle of trying to find out what Leslie unearthed that made her tell you her life might be in danger before we do anything else. Don't you think Rose has been gone a long time?"

With her heart hammering in her throat, Rose scurried through the dining room and managed to be in the kitchen calmly pouring coffee for three when Allan came to see what was taking her so long. Looking at him with a perfectly open face, Rose told him she had been forced to make new coffee because the first potful she made was so strong it was undrinkable. She was beginning to have doubts about Allan again. Oh, she knew he was *the* Allan Holliday, all right, but just because he was a nationally known photographer gave her no assurance that he was not capable of duplicity. Her emotions were mixed. It gave her a feeling of relief to know that she was not going to be all alone in the house that night. It also made her feel better to know that Allan was concerned enough to ask David to have his sister come over. But what if Allan was the one who wanted her house? Had it indeed been a coincidence that Allan's car had been parked right next to Leslie's that night? She could visualize him watching from some concealed place until the girl left the office building. Then he could have gone through his act.

Of course there were other possibilities to consider. Mrs. Hanson seemed a most unlikely suspect to Rose in spite of what Allan had said. Even so, she found herself exploring the idea as the Hansons came in and sat down in the kitchen. Jim was such a mild man. It was almost impossible for her to consider Jim Hanson in the role of a villain. Then there was David Dedrick. Rose knew people were not always what they appeared to be on the surface, but even though she could not find it in her heart to really suspect David Dedrick, she had to consider it. In the back of her mind was the almost bearlike figure of Mitchell LeBlanc. Could Mitch and Veronica really have reason for wanting her house, in spite of the worthlessness of her early theory? She knew if she were writing a book about an old house and an attempt by someone to make the old house uninhabitable, she would have to give the house a hidden treasure of some kind. In Virginia City the treasure would have to be gold or silver, but she tended to shrug that idea away, as well as the idea of there being some fabulous Peter Overstock jewels as she'd read in the library. Could it be that Mitch had unearthed something during one of those times he had been so helpful to her? She found herself thinking more and more about that angle as the conversation ebbed and flowed all around her. It piqued her a little to think maybe Mitch's attentions (unwanted as they had been) could have been due to an ulterior motive.

Then there was Doctor Kellerman. The unwanted suitor. Like David, Rose tended to think it must surely be someone she knew who had spirited Leslie away. Under her thoughts and the partial attention she was giving to the talk that was going on in the room, she was conscious of a tentacle of fear for her niece. Soon she would have to call Irene. When she did, at least she could tell her sister the police had been called. What small comfort that would be, she found herself thinking. It would be like telling someone a child had been killed, but death had come suddenly—that at least the child hadn't suffered, and besides, the police had been notified. How much more could she take before she broke? She had fainted when she had heard the ghostly voice. What if someone was determined to drive her out of her mind? Lock her up in an institution somewhere. Oh, Lord. Her imagination was carrying her away again. It was so much easier to write about frightening things than to actually find herself living them. She jumped when the door chimes sounded.

"I'll go," said Allan.

"I'll go with you," said David Dedrick. And it came to Rose that David might be suspicious of Allan, too. Or maybe David suspected that Allan was suspicious of him. And maybe David knew more than he was telling. It could be that David Dedrick didn't want Allan to speak to the police first. She realized with a little pang of remorse that paranoia was an insidious disease. How could she be absolutely sure that she knew what she was doing every minute of her time? There were such things as split personalities. Well, there was no doubt about it, she could allow her mind to run away with her completely if she wanted to.

David and Allan brought the two men into the kitchen. They were Arthur Compton and Larry Banks. Neither was in uniform. They had identification that had apparently satisfied both Allan and David that they were from the office of the Sheriff of Storey County. David knew the younger of the two. He called him by his first name. "Larry, I think you ought to start with statements from everyone concerned." The one called Compton said he thought that was a good idea, but it was obvious from the start that Larry Banks was in command. He had brought alone a tape recorder. With a pleasant smile, he indicated that he would prefer hearing from Rose first. "But before we start recording anything, I think we ought to have an understanding. The missing girl might not be missing after all. A lot of times, a young person just leaves a house without notice. Strictly speaking, unless there is pretty strong evidence of foul play, we can't do much. Mr. Holliday told us the girl vanished without leaving a trace and he further established that she might be in danger of death due to exposure. Now. My first question has to do with the girl's mental state." A concerned expression was in his brown eyes as they rested on Rose's face. "Mrs. Winters, would you prefer telling me what you know about your niece in another room?"

Rose thought about Phillip, and the marriage that didn't take place. She wasn't at all sure Leslie had mentioned anything to David Dedrick about her shattered romance, and that alone was cause enough to prompt her to nod her head in the affirmative.

"Perhaps we could go into the library. I work in there, and it's quite warm, which is more than I can say for the kitchen." Her feet were like chunks of ice. There was a draft on the kitchen floor that she would have to look into.

When she seated Larry Banks at her desk and took the chair across from it, she felt that sensation of unreality again. It just didn't seem possible to be taking part in an interview concerning Leslie's disappearance. Besides, it was not at all the way she had thought it would be. There was no smart looking young stenographer, the officer was not in uniform and she didn't even know whether she should address him as Sergeant, Lieutenant, Deputy or what. Things in Storey County were rather informal, she felt. But informal or not, she had an idea that Larry Banks would be thorough. His voice was mild when he began to question her.

"When was the last time you saw your niece, Mrs. Winters?"

"This morning."

"Will you state the circumstances, please?"

"Yes. I awakened in Leslie's room. I slept in the other twin bed last night."

"Do you usually share Miss Ellison's bedroom?"

"No. Something unusual has been taking place around here. Frightening, actually."

"What had happened to frighten you?"

The tape recorder made a barely discernible humming sound. She told him about the lights going out, the eerie voice, and finally the mouse or whatever it was that ran across Leslie's foot and the noise she had heard in the laundry room. "Leslie was exhausted and I thought it best to share her room."

"These voices that were heard, had they been heard before in this house?"

"If they were, I didn't hear them. Mrs. Hanson told me on several different occasions that she always heard the strange words when the lights went off. When the electricity failed. Which usually happens when the wind is up."

"I see. But you had not heard any voice until recently. Is that right?"

"That's right. You see, I keep rather early hours. As a general rule, I go to bed before ten o'clock because I like to get up early and start writing. Most of my work is done before two o'clock in the afternoon. I *have* noticed how often the power fails. My typewriter is electric. When it doesn't work, I tend to get upset. But I always have some research to do, so I usually do that during the time the electricity is off."

"When you are writing, do you keep the door closed, Mrs. Winters?"

"Yes, I do. It's a habit I developed when I first started writing. You see, people tend to believe when a person works at home, the work isn't important. I not only close the door to the library, but I lock it. I try to maintain a strict writing schedule and unless an emergency arises I refuse to be interrupted."

"Very well. Now about the missing young lady— you last saw your niece this morning, you said."

"Yes. She went to work. She drove back home and put her car in the garage."

"She works in Carson City?"

"Yes. In the Bureau of Vital Statistics."

"And after she went to work?"

"I went into my own bedroom early in the

170

morning. Mr. Holliday had put the coffee pot in my room. After I bathed and dressed I went downstairs and started to write as soon as I'd had breakfast. Mr. Holliday returned at somewhere close to eleven and we went to Reno."

"Were you gone all day?"

"Yes. We went to the library. We . . . ah, wanted to look into the past history of the house. We returned to the house and my niece had disappeared."

"Tell me what you can about your niece's disappearance."

Drawing a long and unsteady breath, Rose related the events that had led up to the time that Allan Holliday had called the office of the Storey County Sheriff. When she stopped talking, the room was silent except for the faint humming of the tape recorder. Larry Banks looked at her and smiled. "Do you have any theory at all about this?"

Rose hesitated. During the split second, she realized that she had so many theories that if she told them all to this young man with the mild voice and the nice eyes he would have to come to the conclusion that she was slightly unbalanced.

"Even a far-fetched theory, Mrs. Winters."

"No. I have no idea."

"Mrs. Winters, do you think your niece is, uh, unstable in any way?"

"Of course not. Why do you ask?"

"I was thinking of suicide. I'm sorry, Mrs. Winters, but in a case like this where we don't know anything at all, we have to take everything into consideration."

XIII

After Rose had told Larry Banks all she could, Mary Hanson went in. Then Jim Hanson, David Dedrick, and lastly, Allan. Arthur Compton spent the time that his partner took in interviews by going over every inch of the house. He said he would swear that, to the best of his knowledge, there was no way to get in or out of the house except the conventional way. Doors and windows. "I've looked in every conceivable place as well as the less common places."

"There's a basement?" asked Larry Banks. They were once again in the kitchen.

"Yes, sir. There's a basement with a back stairs and a side entrance. The one at the back appears to have been built much earlier than the one at the side. It's been boarded up for some time. That is, you can see the steps all right, but the little set of double doors at the top has been locked and several other pieces of planking have been nailed over them. Some kind of pottery is arranged over the place where the doors are on the outside." Compton looked at Rose. "Isn't it pottery?"

"Yes. There were several varieties of evergreen in the pots when I came here. They were root bound, so I had them set out on the property. I thought the pottery containers were too old and rare to throw away, so I kept them."

"They *are* rare," said David Dedrick. "Early Redware, mostly. And I believe a Bennington piece or two. Mother mentioned them. She's a pottery freak."

"Well, they look as if they haven't been disturbed for a long time," said Compton. His eyes darted from David to Rose to Larry Banks and then to Allan. "I found something very strange on the bottom step of the basement steps that are used all the time." He reached in his pocket and brought out a white tissue. When he opened it, a gold ring sparkled under the lights. "Does this look like a ring you've seen before, Mrs. Winters?"

"I don't have to look at it closely," said Rose. "That's Leslie's high school graduation ring. It will have the words, Stonehaven High School, 1978 on it. She always wears that ring."

"Was she wearing it today?"

Rose nodded. "I'm sure she was. It was always on her hand. I asked her one day if she ever took it off, and she said only to clean it."

"In that case, I would tend to believe the girl has been in the basement, and since the ring was in the tissue . . . was it, Arthur?" Banks looked at the other officer.

"Yes. It was in the tissue. Otherwise, I would have wrapped it in a handkerchief." He sniffed. "It's a scented tissue. It's the same color, with a blue printed border, as the box in Miss Ellison's bedroom and another box in the bathroom. I'd say the girl dropped it deliberately, hoping it would be found. She probably wrapped it for two reasons: One, because white shows up pretty well and Two, in order to deaden the sound when she dropped it."

"That would mean that she was taken to the basement," said David, "in which case I think we should conduct a thorough search down there."

"But Officer Compton has searched the basement," said Allan.

"Yes," David agreed, "but Mrs. Hanson said she looked all over the house. She didn't see the tissue with the ring in it. I don't think anyone would mind looking it over again. We should all go down and have a look. Different people tend to look at different things. And *for* different things, too."

Mary Hanson said she had been looking for Leslie, not some small object such as a tissue. Besides, she added, her eyes were not too good.

"Exactly," said David. "A trained representative of the law would look at every available surface, not necessarily for Leslie, but for anything. I would be more likely to look for Leslie too. But Mrs. Winters knows the basement pretty thoroughly. There could be some places that Sergeant Compton has missed."

"It certainly couldn't hurt anything," said Larry Banks.

"Oh, the poor, dear girl," said Mary Hanson. "And to think, she was probably right down there in the basement with somebody holding a hand over her mouth while I was down there calling her name. I didn't even turn on the light in the coal room. We had it filled last week and I know it's overflowing.

They put in too much the last time and I meant to tell them to not bring so much this time because when Jim opened the door it came tumbling out on him. I forgot about it. But now I'm almost afraid to go down there and look because of what we might find." Her worried eyes met Rose's blue ones.

Rose shuddered, trying to erase a sudden vision of one of Leslie's long legs sticking out from under a pile of coal.

Allan cleared his throat and said, "I, ah, I don't believe anyone has mentioned this, but Mr. Banks is Lieutenant Banks, and the other officer is Sergeant Compton. I suppose everyone knew, since David did."

Rose thought of how shocked she had been when she first visited a doctor in his office in the west. She had never seen a professional man in anything other than a dark business suit, white shirt and tie. The doctor she had gone to see about a throat infection had been wearing a yellow sports shirt, opened at the neck. Her thoughts were interrupted just as she was thinking a uniform doesn't make a good officer any more than a dark suit controls the quality of a doctor's diagnosis, when the door chimes rang.

"I'll go," said Allan.

A little shard of anger pricked Rose's mind. "Thank you," she said coldly. "I'll answer the door." After all, it was her home. She felt she had a right to answer the door if she chose to.

"I believe I will accompany you, Mrs. Winters," said the younger of the two officers. "It's rather doubtful, but there is a slim chance that a note from a kidnapper might be delivered. I'd like to have a chance to see the person who brings the note, if such should be the case."

Dizzily, Rose got to her feet. For a second the kitchen table whirled around along with all the people who were gathered around it. She hadn't thought of kidnapping.

Doctor Kellerman stood on the porch. He lifted his hat in a courtly manner and gave Rose a sympathetic smile. "I've heard the news about your niece. I came to see if there is anything I can do."

"Come in, please," said Rose. She was deeply touched by the doctor's offer. His hand was warm on her shoulder as he touched her lightly, indicating by his very presence that he was with her in her time of need. But just as she finished the introductions all around, she was stabbed with a significant thought. Although she'd discarded Doctor Kellerman as a suspect in the ghost business, his offer for her house and the grounds seemed almost too pat. Could it be Doctor Kellerman who had been in the house when she and Allan drove up? Doctor Kellerman who had stood in the doorway with his arms held high—a big, threatening figure in the partial darkness? He was certainly big enough, she decided. Doctor Kellerman stood well over six feet tall. With his heavy jacket, he appeared much heavier than he actually was. In size, the doctor was almost the same as Mitch LeBlanc. David Dedrick was around five ten and very slender. Allan Holliday was about two inches taller, but Allan was not heavy across the chest or wide in the shoulders as were both Mitchell LeBlanc and Doctor Kellerman. In the dark, she realized, any figure that stood tall and looming would appear bigger, though. Without being too obvious about it, she looked at Kellerman's feet. They were big. Bigger than Mrs. Hanson's, visible from where the cook sat sideways

176

at the table, both feet on the floor under her chair.

"We were about to go to the basement, Doctor," said Allan Holliday. He was being extraordinarily courteous, almost too affable as he asked the doctor if he would like to go along, explaining about the ring found by Sergeant Compton. It rather amused Rose, who had always halfway thought it would be exciting to have men vying for her attention. Once she had told Mark about her secret yearning, saying the desire to be desirable was no doubt a holdover from her frustrated youth. Mark had found her remark highly delightful, and he had also informed her that in his opinion anyone who preferred Irene over Rose was slightly out of it.

As they all trooped to the basement she realized she had again thought of Mark, but with a difference. The bittersweet longing for him was no longer with her. Allan Holliday had changed all that. How terrible it would be if it turned out that Allan was the one who was behind everything! She could hardly bear to contemplate that possibility, even though she had tried, all along, to be unprejudiced in her judgment. At least she was certain Allan had been with her at the time of Leslie's disappearance— but she had to consider that he could have a confederate. She hoped not.

"To the left here is the laundry room," she said as she got to the bottom of the stairs. Her right hand found the light switch.

David Dedrick had a white ring around his mouth. His hands were shaking as he went to the basket of clothing and ran through the garments and towels with his hands. Rose wondered what he would have done if anything had been in that basket besides the clothes. A sick feeling was in the pit of her stomach, yet she had watched, horrified, when the boy had stepped forward and reached into the basket up to his elbows. She had known exactly what had been on his mind.

Compton spoke up. "I didn't think of that." There was an honest note of admiration in his voice.

They went to the root cellar and saw nothing there except the few dusty boxes on the floor and a bushel of potatoes and a half bushel of apples. The room was kept cold. No heat penetrated from the coal furnace as long as the door was shut.

"Right there is where I found the girl's class ring," said Compton. He pointed toward the bottom step and everybody looked. "He could have gone right up those stairs and out on the sidewalk as soon as he thought the coast was clear. He could have put something over the girl's mouth to keep her from crying out."

"Or he could have drugged her," said Doctor Kellerman.

"Or knocked her out," added David grimly. "Leslie isn't a fragile little girl. I have an idea she gave somebody pretty much of a scrap unless something was done to her right away to keep her from fighting and yelling."

"The furnace room is in here," said Rose, fighting waves of nausea. "Watch your step. There's a step down and it isn't easy to see in this light." Waving her arm to take in the vastness of the furnace room, she explained that the root cellar and the laundry room had been built later, when an addition had been made to the house. "There's nothing here but the furnace, the little wine cellar to the right, and beyond the door that leads to the wine cellar is the coal room. That door there to the left leads to the upstairs, but as Sergeant Compton explained, it is no longer in use."

Lieutenant Banks opened the door to the coal bin. It made a scraping, screaming sound as the bottom of the door grated against little slivers of coal.

"Oh, dear!" cried Mrs. Hanson.

Her husband spoke up hurriedly. "Now, sweetheart, you know for sure nobody could have put a girl under there without making a lot of noise. Surely you or I would have heard it. Leslie disappeared sometime between the time she went upstairs and the time the lights went out. You realized it right off. Then Mrs. Winters came home, and all of it happened in the space of about three minutes. I wouldn't give it a thought, because Mrs. Winters and Mr. Holliday would certainly have heard the noise of the door opening or closing. It makes a fierce sounding noise upstairs when I fill the automatic fireman."

"That's right," said Rose. Noises from the basement carried all through the house, as she and Allan already knew.

Allan pointed out that there had been no footprints in the snow when he had looked outside. "Nothing recent, anyway."

"How can you tell if a snow print is recent or not?" asked David.

"It has to do with a look of freezing, then melting, then freezing again," Allan explained.

David was openly hostile for the first time. With clenched fists, he stood under the harsh bulb that hung shadeless overhead. "We have only your word for that, Mr. Holliday."

"Look," said Allan. "I was with Mrs. Winters at the time Leslie disappeared."

"True enough, but you could have somebody working with you."

"I don't think it's quite the time for us to jump to any conclusions, make any accusations," said Larry Banks in his mild voice. "We don't even know the girl is missing. I would say it does look suspicious on the surface, but she could be almost anywhere, doing almost anything, and all for reasons of her own, because she wants to. She might come home at any minute, absolutely amazed that she's caused all this furor."

"We had a date," reminded David of anybody who was interested. "Leslie isn't in the habit of being discourteous. She's probably one of the most thoughtful and considerate girls I've ever known. Besides, she told me she'd discovered something that made her afraid. She said her life might be in danger." David took a step forward. His eyes blazed.

"We have only your word for that," said Allan Holliday sharply.

"Are you calling me a liar, old man?"

"No, but you said the same thing about foot tracks in the snow," Allan answered.

"Oh, shut up," said Doctor Kellerman. "In the first place, young man, nobody in this room is old. You're just young, and that's the difference. To you, everybody beyond the age of thirty is old, according to what I hear."

Mrs. Hanson laughed nervously, mirthlessly.

The laugh broke off in the middle when Sergeant Compton spoke. "I also didn't look in the furnace. I couldn't figure a way to get the door open. It was easy enough to look inside the little door that shows how much coal is in the automatic fireman. There isn't much."

"Look *inside* the furnace?" Rose stared at the licking yellow flames that were visible inside the old-fashioned isinglass of the door. She put her hands up to her face and covered her eyes as if to blot out the ghastly vision that had been in front of her. Leslie could not be—nobody would be so cruel as to put her in that roaring inferno!

"The door is a little tricky to open," said Jim Hanson. His face was pale as he walked slowly toward the furnace. Mrs. Hanson moved closer to Rose. Gently, she touched her arm.

"Don't you think we should go upstairs, Mrs. Winters?"

Doctor Kellerman's voice suddenly boomed forth. "Yes. By all means, you ladies go upstairs."

"If she's in there," said Rose in a strangled voice, "then I've got to know it sooner or later." Mr. Hanson fumbled with the latch at the door, at the same time he pulled out he had to lift up. The metal door yawned open and the flames instantly roared outward.

XIV

An hour later, Rose consented to staying upstairs
with the cook while the men went downstairs to look
at what remained in the furnace. The flames had
been too high, the fire too hot for them to see anything for a while. The lieutenant had shut off the
automatic feeder and the house was growing quite
cold. Once again, Rose had put off calling her sister.
Her nerves were taut. On edge from the strain of
waiting, of worrying and thinking about the remains
of her niece, burning in that big old-fashioned furnace. She wished she had not listened when Doctor
Kellerman had been asked how much of a human
being could be expected to remain intact after it had
been subjected to that kind of intense heat. The
doctor had not gone into gruesome details, but his
flat statement of fact had been enough. "Dental
work. Gold bridges, platinum or silver. Some bones,
possibly. Any jewelry that was made of valuable
metals. Costume jewelry melts quickly."

Mrs. Hanson sat with folded hands, silently. Rose

sat on the edge of a chair. Each woman seemed to be holding her breath as they listened to the sounds coming from below. It was warm in the kitchen because someone had lit the oven in the stove. Someone else had lit the fires in the three fireplaces on the first floor in order to keep the house from freezing. There was the unmistakable sound of a shovel going into the bowels of the furnace, the ring of metal on metal and then a dumping sound that Rose identified as ashes going into the ash cans. Shifting slightly in her chair, the cook spoke in a near whisper. "I pray to God they don't find anything."

Rose nodded. She couldn't bring herself to answer.

Mrs. Hanson said, "If it hadn't been for those telephone lines being cut, I'd still be hoping Leslie just left the house. But when you consider those lines being chopped off like that, and then that policeman finding her class ring—"

It was taking a long time. Rose tried not to think about tooth fillings and jewelry and how long it would take to turn living tissue to ash. But the sick knowledge was there, in her thoughts, overriding all the other things that filled her mind. Chief place in her thoughts was the pressure of knowing she would soon have to call Irene.

The men came upstairs. Their hair was dusty and Jim Hanson had ashes all the way up to his armpits. "There was nothing," said Lieutenant Compton.

"Then she isn't in there," said Rose. She felt suddenly weak and weary. No words she could say would express the profound relief she felt.

After the officers left, David's sister, Lou Ann, came to the house, Doctor Kellerman left, and the

183

Hansons went to their cottage. Doctor Kellerman held Rose's hand for what seemed to her a very long time and begged her to let him know if he could do anything. "Anything at all, my dear."

When the door had closed behind Doctor Kellerman, Rose said, "It doesn't seem to me that there is any kind of plan for an investigation."

"Oh, but there is. It's just that nothing much can be done tonight," David replied. His sister was putting her coat back on because Rose had asked her to walk to the Hansons' cottage with her so she could use the telephone. The policemen were still out walking around in the snow when she and Lou Ann sprinted across the path that led to the cottage and Rose felt a little better.

It took only a minute for the call to get through to San Francisco. Irene answered right away. She seemed surprised that Rose would call her again so soon. The surprise in her voice soon turned to shock, then disbelief. She said some things that didn't make much sense at first and Rose knew her sister was taking those few seconds to collect herself. Then she said she'd take the next available plane.

"I don't know what you can do," said Rose, "but you'll feel better if you're here."

"At least I can comfort you," said Irene. "No matter what happens, you mustn't blame yourself, Rose." How like Irene it was to remember the other person, to be aware of someone else's feelings, Rose thought, even at a time like that.

"I'll let you go, then, so you can make plane reservations."

"I probably won't have time to call and let you know when I'll arrive, so I'll just take a cab from the

Reno airport," Irene said and started to hang up when Rose stopped her.

"Wait!" She didn't even realize she had been thinking of what she was about to say, but the thought must have been there, hidden in the recesses of her subconscious mind. "Irene, remember those old papers and things you found when you first inherited the Overstock house in San Francisco?"

"Yes. What about them?" Her sister's voice now sounded impatient, anxious to end the conversation and get her reservations taken care of.

"If you still have them, bring them along, will you? They may be very important."

"I didn't destroy them . . . but it'll take a while to remember where I put them. What do you mean, they might be very important?"

"I don't know exactly. But Leslie told David Dedrick that she had come across something important, something that made her believe her life might be in danger. Those papers you have might be a connection of some kind." Now that she had said it, she felt a little foolish. But on the other hand, the slightest bit of knowledge might help tremendously.

When Lou Ann and Rose returned to the big house, the stars were so bright they seemed almost to be exploding in the sky. They spoke of that and made other small talk until the time passed and they could think about going to bed. David and Allan had deccided to sleep downstairs on the sofas. Rose could easily see that it was a toss-up as far as suspicions went. David was suspicious of Allan and Allan was suspicious of David. Under any other circumstances, Rose would have been deeply engrossed in the play of human emotions, but she was too much aware of her own doubts. Actually, she suspected both of them and everyone else.

When they were upstairs in Leslie's room and Rose had changed the sheets and pillow cases for Lou Ann, the girl looked out of the upstairs window and drew in her breath sharply. "What's that? It looks like something burning."

"Oh, that's the site of the other Overstock house," Rose said. She went to the window and looked out. "Probably you don't see so much of the column of steam from your house, because of the hill. I remember how alarmed I was when I first saw that. It's one of those underground hot springs, you know. That house was heated by the captured steam. This one didn't have the underground springs. It does look as if the place is on fire, doesn't it? But it isn't. In very cold weather, the steam seems to condense more rapidly. When the stars are bright and there's a full moon, it looks very eerie."

Lou Ann shuddered. "Is there anything left of the other house? I didn't even know there was one."

"Lou Ann, you've probably heard the old story and forgotten about it. At seventeen, other things are in the foreground and local history gets pushed into the background, even forgotten about. And that's the way it should be. No, nothing's left but the basement. According to people I've talked with, the house didn't burn to the ground, but it was uninhabitable. It was finally razed, as a safety measure. A chimney was still standing when I first came to look at this place, but it's since been torn down. Small boys, I imagine. Or maybe the chimney was undermined by the constant winds."

Without warning, the lights went out. Lou Ann

Dedrick gasped. "They do this now and then," said Rose. "Just stay where you are and I'll get a candle."

During the small silence when Rose was looking for a candle, a high wind rose outside. "A Washoe Zephyr," cried Lou Ann. "I hate it when the wind blows. It's destructive and mindless."

There was a high, keening sound to it, almost like a human being in abject misery. It wailed and moaned through the trees outside the window and then it was still for a second. Then the whispered sound of the voice Rose had come to dread came creeping into the room. "Help, Becky. Help me." Chills broke out on her arms and on the back of her neck.

In the flickering light from the candle she still held in her shaking hand, she saw Lou Ann turn around and look at her with wide eyes. "Did you hear that?"

"Yes, I heard it."

"It's supernatural!" The girl's eyes grew wider. Her mouth was open in fear.

"I don't know," said Rose slowly. "I just don't know. If you're afraid, I could get David to take you back to your house."

The lights came on as suddenly as they had gone off. Lou Ann, looking a little ashamed, said she was not afraid. The girl and then the woman prepared for bed and after a while they turned the lights out in the room and Lou Ann went to sleep. Listening to the sound of her deep breathing, Rose envied the young girl. She had an idea sleep would never come to her. She couldn't get herself to settle down. Instead, she thought about her sister, wondering when she would arrive. And she tried not to wonder and worry about Leslie. Constructive thinking was not the wasted motion and emotion of fruitless worry. She knew that, and kept telling herself that, but everywhere she turned she found herself in a quandary, trying to pull things together and make some kind of sense out of them.

The nightsounds of the house grew louder and louder to her wide awake senses. She could hear creakings of the floorboards that she had not noticed before. The wind had died a little, but it still shrieked and howled with an almost human quality. The windows rattled and a frozen branch rubbed against the house somewhere. The shadows in the room were dense and black, relieved by bright patches of moonlight. Sometimes the shadows seemed to move. Everything seemed to be closing in on her. She listened to the grandfather clock as it chimed one, then one-thirty, then two and two-thirty. When it struck three o'clock she was sitting on the edge of the bed, thinking of a cup of hot chocolate to help her sleep. Throwing a robe over her nightgown and slipping her feet into bedroom slippers, she crept silently from the room. Allan and David had left a night light on. The hall was dim, but the stairs were quite bright. She felt very strange as she walked by the two sleeping men on the sofas. Allan moaned a little in his sleep and David sighed as she stealthily walked on tiptoe around them. A smile quirked at the corners of her lips. She would chide them gently in the morning. They had elected to sleep downstairs in order to keep an eye on things. She had an idea she could move the two sofas, complete with sleeping men, and neither of them would be the wiser. The refrigerator door seemed very loud because she was trying to be so quiet. She hadn't realized how much noise it made when the door opened before. When she took the milk out and reached for the can of instant chocolate, she happened to look out the window and then was when the thought struck her.

"Why not?" She whispered the two words and felt a quickening of her heart. "Yes!" It was at least possible. Maybe she should awaken Allan or David. But wait . . . wouldn't it be better to do it herself? How did she know either Allan or David was sleeping there for her protection? How could she know for sure that one of them was not there to see that she didn't go prowling around on her own property. To watch her, instead of to protect her.

Of course she would be afraid.

And she couldn't go out in the cold with nothing on but a flimsy bathrobe and a pair of bedroom slippers.

But there were the back stairs, which she had forgotten all about when she came downstairs. She could go up to her own room the back way, get out some heavy slacks, a coat, shoes and boots, gloves—and in the middle of the night like this, nobody would miss her. And nobody would think Rose Winters was capable of undertaking a journey such as she was contemplating, either. Not at three o'clock in the morning! The hot chocolate was a good idea, too. It would fortify her against the cold. Maybe bolster her courage. She would turn the milk on low while she hurried upstairs and slipped into warm clothes. Then she would drink a cup of hot chocolate and leave, silently.

If she hadn't lost her courage when she got back downstairs, she told herself grimly.

But she wasn't going to lose her courage. Through

her mind went something like a slow motion film. Leslie as a darling little baby, all cuddly and sweet, smelling of Mennen's baby powder, fresh from her bath. How she had envied her sister. How she had loved to cuddle the baby close to her own chest. She had always thought if she ever had a baby it might look something like Leslie. But then she had not ever had a child of her own. She saw pictures of Leslie, toddling and falling on her round little bottom, laughing delightfully, just learning to walk. Irene had been ill at about that time and Rose and Mark had taken Leslie to their house and kept her for a few months while Irene recovered. Holidays, several weeks out of the summer and sometimes just for weekends, Leslie had often come to visit Rose and Mark.

Although she was trembling from head to foot, she managed to get into a pair of woolen slacks, a long sleeved sweater and a heavy hooded coat in a hurry, all without making a sound. Gloves were in her coat pocket. Walking shoes and rubber boots were on her feet when she sneaked down the back steps. *Leslie, if you're there, I'm coming.* She added the chocolate mixture to the hot milk and drank it quickly. *Leslie, I'm coming!* Why hadn't she thought of that place earlier?

Because she had been in a state of shock, she supposed. Numb. Unable to think constructively.

Even when Lou Ann Dedrick had asked her about the billows of steam that were rising into the air she hadn't thought about the other house. It now seemed almost as if she had deliberately been keeping herself from remembering about the door not too far from the kitchen that opened onto a flight of ancient stairs. The stairs led into the tunnel.

It took all her strength to pull the trap door open by the rusty old iron ring. "What's this?" Leslie had asked, shortly after she had come to the house to live. It had been unseasonably warm that day.

"Oh, that's a trap door." Rose remembered how Leslie had looked that bright sunny afternoon, how brimming with youthful enthusiasm.

"Where does it lead to?"

"Across to the other house. The one that used to be there before fire took it partly down and then the rest of it was leveled. Brothers had these houses built. I've always wondered if this was part of a temporary mine shaft. Otherwise, why would the tunnel be here?"

"Maybe there was a little hanky panky going on," Leslie had answered. "You know, between the other brother and his wife or something. I'm told today's youth are not the first young people to discover sex." Leslie had bent down just as Rose was doing right then, and pulled at the iron ring. The ground had not been frozen all around it that day and covered over with snow as it now had been for three days, and the door had come open rather easily. Leslie had stared down into the darkness and made a face. "Ugh! Bats and things. Maybe rats might even be down in there." She had closed the door with a bang. "Who told you the tunnel led to the other house?"

"Mitchell LeBlanc."

"Damn!" The door was frozen quite fast to the ground. Rose tugged with all her might and was able to barely budge it. She looked around for something to pry into the inch or so that she had worked loose. The flashlight in her hand was icy cold and the wind was howling in the trees overhead, but she found a big stick that looked substantial enough. In her heavy clothes, she was sweating with exertion when she finally managed to open the door. But her hands were clumsy with the cold. As she descended to the first and then the second step, she felt a rush of rank smelling air coming up at her. But it was warmer down there than it was on the surface. Should she close the door behind her? For a moment, she stood there uncertainly on the second step down. A cold wave of terror that had nothing to do with the solid snow on either side of her head washed over her. What if she did close the door, and what if she wanted to get out of there quickly? How could she manage to pry up on the door if it froze shut again? She shuddered. It would be like being buried alive. No. Best not to close the door after her.

The flashlight cast a round yellow beam straight ahead as she stood on the bottom step, thankful she had navigated the uneven and rotting boards without falling. Overhead, solid timbers and silvered woodgrain were chunked together. She wondered if they were two by fours, four by sixes or bigger. Some day she'd ask somebody. The same rough-hewn lumber formed the sides of the tunnel. What was she walking on? The yellow beam went down to her feet and she saw what looked like a solid dirt path with little slivers of coal and cinder imbedded in it. What if the path fell through with her? What if the top caved in on her? And it was dark. Black as pitch except for the glaring yellow light she was shining along the floor of the tunnel. What if the batteries decided to fail? Rose had never had much luck with flashlights. Her father had accused her of casting a hex on the batteries and Mark had said she often forgot to turn them off after using them.

Something fluttered around her feet. A toad, maybe. Stepping gingerly, she shone the light back down and saw something small and bright slither away. A lizard, perhaps. Or a snake. Of course not a snake! They hibernated this time of year, didn't they? Her hand was shaking so hard that the light jiggled up and down. Now she wished she had closed the door after her. The wind was strong in the cave. No doubt it was entering the open door and being sucked along through the tunnel where it was open at the other end. At least she hoped it would be open at the other end.

Wisps of hair came loose and blew across her eyes. She brushed them back with cold fingers inside their gloves and cleared her vision in time to see a huge spiderweb swaying directly overhead. Stifling a scream, she ducked big dark flapping wings that were swooping down on her. An owl? In her numbed mind she recalled having read of owls that attacked people in Germany. A shrill cry sounded above the roar of the wind. She kept her head down low, trying to protect it with her one free hand, the light illuminating a tunnel within the tunnel where she was now inching her way along. Something at her feet made her lose her footing and stumble a little, but she didn't fall. Gasping, she looked down and saw the track, narrow and partially hidden by accumulated silt and debris. Funny. She had forgotten all about the tracks they had carried the ore on. She didn't recall having seen it at the beginning of the tunnel, but it was probably covered all the way over

193

back there. *Back there!* She knew she couldn't have traveled far. Grimly, she glanced at the blackness behind her, but only for an instant. She knew if she thought about how far thirty yards was she would be tempted to run back to the relative safety of the open trap door. Some rock piles were directly in front of her. Not too many, but enough to cause her to flash the light up again, apprehensively. Was the shored-up roof about to give way? Her mind seemed to float to the top of the tunnel, to test and judge the amount of rock and earth and old timbers that might come falling down on her at any minute. How many feet would it take to completely bury her?

Think about something else, she commanded herself. Something glistened a few feet ahead and she saw that it was water. A small underground spring, fed from God knew where. Under the light, the water sparkled. Tiny drops bounced off rocks and spilled over the side of the lodge, making the floor wet in spots where she walked. A coiled snake eyed her sluggishly and she felt a tremor shake her from head to toe as she side-stepped it. Why had she come? Why had she come alone? Because she couldn't trust anybody. That was why she had come alone, she answered herself wearily. But she could have waited until daylight. But no she couldn't. Because if there was a chance that Leslie was inside that tunnel somewhere—or in the basement of the house that had burned—she knew time was important. Even so, she wished she had not started. Now she was too terrified to turn back.

A new wave of horror rolled over her, causing her heart to thump in her chest. The wind was no longer rushing through the tunnel. Her hair seemed to rise up and stand straight up under her hood. Since the wind was no longer being sucked through the interior of the narrow tunnel, that meant only one thing: someone had shut off the opening at one end or another. If somebody had been lurking outside her house—if someone had seen her come out and go down the steps after she finally got the trap door open—her mouth was dry at the thought. A metallic taste was on her tongue and she understood the meaning of the actual *taste* of terror. Certainly there was another way to get to the burned-out house. What was to keep someone from plowing through the snow drifts that lay over the place she was precariously inching her way through? How could she be sure somebody was not, right this minute, closing off the other opening? A jutting boulder to her right made her scream. It looked exactly like a man's face in the dimming light of the flashlight she carried. The sound of the scream echoed back to her, mocking her. There was no way out of the situation except one, and she wasn't sure of that one way, but she collected herself and told herself sternly to put one foot in front of the other and keep going. And not to think about the batteries dying.

A rustling sound close to her ear made all her senses wildly alive for one heart-stopping instant of alertness. Something whispered, or was it spinning through the air? She had time to barely wonder, and then she knew. There was the impact of something against the side of her head. As she went down, she thought with a certain amount of dazed clarity, *I'm not alone in here. Probably never have been.*

XV

First she dreamed she was in a wagon of some kind, or maybe it was a carriage. Whatever conveyance she was in, she knew a moment of displeasure because apparently the thing had hit a deep rut. She was jostled about without mercy. Further, the seat was not at all comfortable. Somebody was talking to her in an even tone of voice. Now and then she could make out her name and she supposed whoever it was doing the talking intended to be reassuring, but she was far from reassured. It was dark as a night without moon or stars and she was stiff with cold. It would be nice if she could get out of that dream. Sometimes when she had bad dreams, she could bring forth a tremendous effort and turn herself over in bed, but this time she couldn't. Strong hands were holding her down. She made a little noise of protest, wishing she could see, because suddenly she realized she was not having a dream at all. An orange slash of fear centered in the middle of her mind and panic seized her. She had always been afraid of losing her mind. Had that happened to her now? Was she confined in a straight jacket, being transported to some dismal padded cell? She wanted to tell them—or him—she wasn't insane, it was just that her head hurt so terribly and she couldn't see. "Listen, I—" She began to speak and felt the person stumble.

"Easy," he said. "Just take it easy. I'll soon have you out of here."

Other sensations began to penetrate her dim consciousness. The person who was carrying her was having difficulty with his breathing. A woolen coat or jacket, or maybe it was a blanket, was rough against her cheek. She felt the coarsely woven material as the person stumbled, went almost all the way down and then righted himself. And she knew it was a man. Knew it by the voice. The voice which was at that moment muttering, "Damn it!"

Searchingly, she tried to place that voice. She knew her very life might depend on placing the voice, because now she remembered the entire thing. The tunnel that led from her own house to the basement of the other Overstock house. Yes. She had not been able to sleep. She had thought about the tunnel, the trap door in the yard that was covered over with snow, then she had dressed, had some hot chocolate and finally managed to get the door open. Then all those frightening things. And the flashlight had grown dimmer and dimmer. An alarm bell seemed to jangle through her head as she remembered the terror that had gripped her there at the last when she had realized she was not alone in the tunnel. Now she felt positive that her assailant was carrying her out of there, knowing that sooner or later someone would think of that tunnel. After all,

Virginia City was a maze of old tunnels underground. Sometimes the earth shifted and the ground above caved in. Yes, sooner or later, someone would go underground to look for Rose herself, maybe. At least they would think to look for Leslie there. So the man had to get her out of there. Hide her away somewhere. Probably kill her.

"It can't be much farther," he said gently.

All she could think of was the things she wanted to do before she left this world. There were so many things left undone. The books she wanted to write. The one she was currently working on. A new recipe she wanted to try. Or have Mrs. Hanson try, to be truthful. It seemed ridiculous that she would be thinking of such trite things when she knew, or at least felt, that she didn't have much longer to live. She ought to be thinking about a way out. In a flash it came to her that there probably was no way out for her. But she was willing to try. If she pretended to be dazed, out of touch, perhaps she could gain a few more precious minutes. Maybe she could trick the man who was carrying her out of there into believing she was temporarily out of her mind, then trick him, watch for her chance to escape.

"Darling, I can see a glimmer of light."

Darling! Now she recognized his voice all right. He had called her darling before. Earlier that night? It seemed ages ago. It must be getting close to daylight, she supposed, so actually he had called her darling the night before, and she—foolish woman that she was—had been thrilled! She deliberately made her voice sound thick and in a wondering voice asked, "George?"

"George?" Allan's voice held a question in it. "I'm not George. I'm Allan Holliday. Who do you know named George?" His arms tightened around her.

Actually, the name had come to Rose without any effort. She had known a lot of Georges in her day, she thought groggily. She had gone to school with one in the fourth grade, as a matter of fact. She had just thought it was as good a name as any to start things off with. Now he was on the steps. She felt his body strain with the effort of making sure of his footing and maintaining his hold on her body. She looked up and saw a misty sky, faintly studded with stars. They were no longer bright because the light of day was beginning to dim their glory. What should she say next to convince him she was out of her head? Something inane. It was difficult to pretend to be stupefied when she really was, at least a little. "Will you turn up the thermostat? It seems very cold here in the library."

He groaned and sagged against the rough timbers at the side of the stairs. Now she could feel the wind on her face and knew it was not far to the top. "Oh, Rose, darling!" he said. He was gasping for breath. That made her feel good. Allan was not used to carrying women around in tunnels. He probably seldom did anything more strenuous than clicking the button on his camera. She didn't weigh much over a hundred pounds, but it hadn't been easy for him to carry her so far. Her head slid down a little and she felt something warm and sticky on her cheek. Then she heard voices from above. As they came out of the stairs, she smelled the harsh stench of kerosene and Jim Hanson's eyes peered at her out of a pale face. The lantern he carried made dancing shadows all around. His wife stood with a black shawl thrown over her head, big, tall and somehow like an avenging black angel. She moved her arms up and down under the shawl and Rose thought of the Fates. The Three Fates. The Goddesses who were supposed to control human life. Which one was she? Clotho? Achesis? Atropos?

"Here. I'll help you," said Jim Hanson, and the enveloping warmth of the black shawl was wrapped around Rose.

"She's got a bad wound on her head," said Allan gravely. "It might be a concussion. She was out like a light when I found her. I don't think she's thinking just right. She called me George." He was helping Mrs. Hanson support her. Something was all out of joint. It was as if Allan had been expecting Mr. and Mrs. Hanson to be there. It was impossible for her to consider that they were all in on some diabolical plot together, yet things were not working out as she had thought they would.

"Poor dear," said Mrs. Hanson. "I think we'd best get her into the house where it's warm, get her stretched out on the sofa. Maybe a nice cup of hot coffee."

Allan again lifted her in his arms. "What we'd better do first is call a doctor. Get him to take a look at this head wound."

"I'm not a child," said Rose firmly.

"Well, you acted like one," said Allan as Mrs. Hanson held the kitchen door open for him. "Why the devil didn't you tell somebody you intended to go out in the middle of the night and search that old tunnel? You almost got yourself killed." He took her into the living room and put her down on the sofa where he had been sleeping when last she saw him. Mrs. Hanson stood over her, wringing her hands.

She said she'd go help Jim into the house, then she'd just go over to her place and call a doctor. "It wouldn't hurt him a bit to have somebody take a look at that ankle of his, anyway," she added with a break in her voice.

"Don't leave me alone with this man!" cried Rose. She stared up into Allan's white face. He stared back at her. Then he dropped to his knees.

"She's afraid of me!" His voice sounded shocked at such an idea.

"You can't get away with it, Allan," Rose heard herself saying. "Whatever it is you want, you can have it, but you can't pretend to make me out as a madwoman and they do away with me."

"It's just the shock," said Mrs. Hanson. "Oh, dear!"

"Call those policemen, too, Mrs. Hanson. That is, if you haven't already done it," said Lou Ann Dedrick. Rose noticed the girl was fully dressed. Her eyes were overflowing with tears. She wondered why everyone was up and around. Then she asked where David was.

"He's—" Lou Ann gulped and broke into wild sobbing. Then she straightened her bent shoulders and pulled herself together. "I did just as you told me, Mr. Holliday. I didn't touch the— I didn't move him or anything. I just couldn't bring myself to leave his body until you got Mrs. Winters out of there."

Rose sat up. Allan pushed her back down, gently. Wildly, she looked from Allan to Lou Ann Dedrick. "Something has happened to your brother. What was it?"

"Somebody killed him," said Lou Ann.

A whistling sound was in Rose's ears. The bright lights in the living room seemed to dance and sway. For the second time in her life she felt herself dropping off the edge of the earth.

XVI

Somebody was saying something about loss of blood, and somebody else was saying something about shock and possible brain concussion, and somebody else mentioned all that horrible discoloration, and Rose knew they were talking about her.

Mrs. Hanson said, "Doctor Kellerman said he'd be here in a matter of seconds and the police are on their way. Listen, don't you think it would be a good idea for me to at least take soap and water and wash that awful looking place on the side of her head?"

"Let the doctor do it," said Allan.

The throbbing pain in Rose's head was a consuming thing. She felt weak and a bit nauseated. It would have been so much easier for her to remain still and give way to the waves of blackness that kept threatening to pull her back down, but she had to know what had happened. She opened her eyes and slowly brought them into focus. Lou Ann was sitting stiffly on the sofa where David had slept, the rumpled bedclothing striking an incongruous note in the growing light of day. Allan was kneeling at her side. She saw a big bloody stain against the front of the coat he was wearing and knew it was her blood, from the wound on her head. Her head seemed to be swelling out of all proportion. It felt as big as a watermelon on the side where something had hit her. Jim Hanson was in a chair, his swollen bare foot propped up on a footstool, his eyes still squinched together with pain. Mrs. Hanson stood in back of him, making wifely sounds.

Rose moved her mouth. It felt stiff and numb. "Tell me what happened," she said in a thick voice that had nothing to do with pretense. "Please. Before Doctor Kellerman gets here. And the police." All she knew for sure was that David Dedrick was dead. In a way, she didn't want to hear. Because it was her fault, she felt sure. But she also knew she couldn't shelter herself from the truth forever. A feeling of hopelessness diffused with sorrow added to her misery. She knew that as long as she lived she would feel responsible for David Dedrick's death. If she hadn't acted so impulsively! If she had been willing to wait until the next day. If she had just been willing to trust someone. So many *ifs*. Then too —if David was dead, there wasn't much hope for Leslie. She felt as if she were living in the throes of a nightmare. Everyone seemed to be talking to her at once, everyone trying to give his own version of what had happened.

After a few minutes, it seemed clear.

Jim Hanson had awakened in the middle of the night because of a charley-horse in his leg. Although Mary had been sleeping at his side, he had not disturbed her. He had stood up and put his weight on the leg that had bothered him and the knotted muscle had stopped hurting, but then he had been unable to get back to sleep. He had decided to go to the bathroom and take a couple of aspirins. While he was in the bathroom, he heard a strange noise. Pushing back the curtains, he saw Rose, just in the act of lifting the door to the steps that led to the tunnel. In the darkness, he had not realized it was his employer. She had worn slacks and a heavy, hooded coat. It was Jim's plan to go around to the front of the big house, skirting the place where he had seen the person opening the door to the tunnel; in that way, he hoped he wouldn't be seen by the intruder. Leaving Mary in bed asleep, Jim took the key to the front door of the main house and went out the side door of the cottage. All was quiet in the house. He assumed everyone was sleeping, and did not want to disturb Rose, who he thought was sleeping upstairs.

David and Allan awakened instantly. Jim described what he had seen and they quickly decided upon a plan of action. Jim, who had once been in the tunnel, would go down there himself. At the same time, David would run the fifty yards to the site of the razed house in an attempt to anticipate the intruder at the other end. Jim explained that the mine tunnel opened into the basement of the other Overstock house, and he expressed self-anger at not having thought of the basement as a place where Leslie might be at that very moment, bound and gagged.

"I just don't know why none of us thought of that, Mrs. Winters," said the older man. "It's been there for as long as I can remember, although I'd only been in the place that one time, with Mitchell LeBlanc. But I know you knew about it, because we'd talked about it. I just didn't think about it until I saw—well, until I saw it was *you*, but I didn't know it was you going down there."

"And you swept all the snow off the sidewalks that led to the opening earlier in the day," said Mrs. Hanson. "That's why there wasn't a sign of a print in the snow."

"Please go on with it," Rose said. She put a tentative hand up to her head and felt clotted blood, but the entire side of her head was numb.

"Then Jim lost his footing," said Allan. "He stumbled. The timbers are jagged and the stairs aren't exactly even. He says he sprained his ankle, but by the looks of it, it might be broken." He looked at his watch. "Where the devil is that doctor?"

"Where were you when Jim fell?" Rose met Allan's eyes.

"Right behind him. He had my flashlight. He said he'd go down first because he knew the lay of the timbers and the steps. He dropped the light when he fell and it went out. I wanted to get him back up on the ground before I went down there. I could tell he was in quite a lot of pain even though he wasn't complaining. It took a long time for me to get him up on the surface. Then I helped him into the cottage and woke Mrs. Hanson."

"Why didn't you call the police right then?"

"We tried to," said Allan. "After all, we all thought at the time that it was an intruder who had gone down into the tunnel. None of us had any idea it was you. We didn't get a dial tone."

"Don't tell me the telephone in the cottage has been put out of order."

"No, it was just a temporary thing. Besides, we

didn't try very long. I've noticed that sometimes you don't always get a dial tone right away, but the telephone didn't seem dead. And Mrs. Hanson said she'd keep trying. You see, right then we heard a shout, then a shot."

Lou Ann Dedrick spoke in a voice flat with controlled emotion. "It was the shot that woke me up. I'm almost sure it was. I think, somehow, I knew it was my brother. Maybe I heard him yell first and even though I was asleep I knew it was David. I turned on the lamp and looked at your bed, Mrs. Winters, and of course it was empty. Then I heard voices outside, people yelling, and looked out the window. I could see Mr. Holliday running across the fields. I didn't know it was Mr. Holliday, of course. I only made out a man's form over there along the ridge, you know where the steam rises up? Well, I thought I saw another man's shape disappear just on the other side of the dip in the land. I'm not sure of it, though. I went downstairs and collided with Mrs. Hanson, who was coming in the kitchen door. She was worried about you, Mrs. Winters."

"Well, I thought the gun shot had probably awakened you, Mrs. Winters," said Mary. "Then this girl said you weren't in your bed. And knowing you, I got to thinking maybe that it was you that went down in that tunnel all alone. I don't mind telling you I was half out of my mind with worry."

"David was—" Allan started to speak then, paused and looked sadly at Lou Ann. "I'm sorry, Miss Dedrick, but with one look at his body I knew he was dead. He was shot at close range, with what I would consider a powerful rifle of some kind. Death was instant, I'm sure. I came back and found out you weren't sleeping. I should have thought to

207

check out your bedroom before I did anything else, Rose. When I realized you were down in that tunnel all alone, possibly about to come face to face with a madman, I'm afraid I didn't think. I just acted. There wasn't time to hunt around for replacements for the flashlight batteries. I grabbed a candle from the kitchen and a few matches and went down. As soon as I lit a match, the wind blew it out. Then I realized after about five matches that sputtered out immediately that the door being open was creating such a draft that the candle would never stay lit once I lighted it. So I went back and closed the door."

"That must have been when the wind stopped roaring through the tunnel," said Rose. "But that was a long time after I was in there."

"It probably just seemed like a long time, darling. It seemed an eternity to me, too."

"But I don't remember seeing a candle when you were carrying me out."

"No. I dropped it. I'm sure you saw the underground spring and the snake. I slipped on a wet rock and lost the candle. The water snuffed it out immediately. I wasn't able to stick my hands down there in the vicinity of that snake. I don't know much about their hibernating habits and I didn't think it was the time to find out. I started striking matches and there was a curve in the tunnel and I thought I could hear your footsteps ahead of me. I just saw your shadow. My God! You looked so small, and so vulnerable. And there was a rock formation that I at first mistook for a man. Then a real man came from directly behind that pile of rocks and I saw, actually saw him hit you with a rock."

Much later, he would tell her how he got to his hands and knees and crawled along the floor of the tunnel, how his hands had come into contact with her body; the way he had recognized her for certain by the feel of her soft hair, the contour of her face, and how he had gently lifted her up and started the long journey back in the pitch black tunnel, all the time in deathly fear that an invisible form would overtake him, tear her from his arms, shoot them both. Right then they were interrupted by the sound of heavy feet on the front porch and the loud knocking at the door along with the insistent ringing of the door chimes.

Doctor Kellerman put his little black bag down on the coffee table a minute later and looked at Rose compassionately. "I understand you've had quite a night of it. Mrs. Hanson, will you get me a basin of warm water and some soap? Don't try to talk; I want to see if you have a fever, Rose." He stuck the thermometer under her tongue and she tasted the bitter wetness of alcohol. Then his hands were on her forehead and two fingers held her eyes wide open while he stared at her pupils. "Hmmm." She wondered why doctors always felt compelled to say that. It told her nothing. Mrs. Hanson was saying something about wanting to wash the wound but Mr. Holliday wouldn't allow it, no, wouldn't hear of it, and everything began to fade a little. The room jerked and spun and at the same time voices seemed grossly loud. Except that she was not quite able to grasp everything that was being said. Words and phrases jumped out at her and others faded off into limbo.

" . . . bad sprain, Jim . . . commission for a while . . ."

"Good boys, Banks and Compton. Hell of it is . . . law into your own hands, seems a shame . . . say he was only twenty-three years old . . . madman."

Lou Ann Dedrick's voice was one she recognized because it was so full of tears. "My parents . . . David was the only boy. But I didn't touch the body, doctor—they told me not to."

Mrs. Hanson came with the basin and cloths. Rose smelled the soft fragrance of her own toilet soap, felt the gentle hands of the doctor as he daubed at her matted hair, wondering all the while in a dazed sort of way if Doctor Kellerman had killed David Dedrick. After all, he had wanted to buy her house. Had offered a good price for it. But how could she be afraid of the man who was tending her wound so gently, gently . . . after all, she had made one stupid mistake after another. To have gone into the tunnel alone, for instance, to say nothing of deciding Allan had been the one, when in all probability he had saved her life.

"Surface wound," said the doctor gruffly. "I won't even have to cut your hair. It's one hell of a bump, yes; but you're lucky. Maybe a small concussion." He slipped the thermometer out of her mouth. Said, "Hmmmm," again. Then, "No fever. Just to be on the safe side, I'll put you on an antibiotic. Your head ache pretty bad, does it?"

She made the mistake of nodding. An anvil chorus started up on the inside of her head and the dizziness came back.

"You just take it easy for a couple of days. I'm sure you'll be all right. I'll give you a couple of pills for the pain. By this time tomorrow you ought to be right as rain. If you still have a lot of pain in your head, give me a call. Jim's going to know he fell down those cussed stairs a lot longer than you're going to know somebody tried to knock your brains out.''

Paper rustled as the doctor shook some white pills out of a packet and asked Mrs. Hanson to get some water. "Better get two glasses. One for your husband.''

"I don't know as I want to go to sleep," said Jim Hanson in a querulous voice.

"This won't make you go to sleep, Jim. It'll just relieve some of that pain in your foot and ankle.'' Everything came into sharp focus again for Rose and she saw Doctor Kellerman cross the room and go over to Lou Ann Dedrick, who still sat in a straight chair with her hands folded in her lap. "Young lady, I don't think you ought to be sitting there in that draft. Besides, I don't like the pallor of your skin.''

"Oh, Doc," Rose said with a tremble in her voice, "it was her brother who was—who was killed.''

Kellerman stopped in front of Lou Ann's chair. He was visibly shaken. "You're Victor Dedrick's daughter? I didn't recognize you.'' He sat down beside the girl and took her small hand in his big bearlike one. "I'm sorry. I can't say how sorry I am. But words . . . they don't amount to much at a time like this, do they? I didn't realize you were here, child. Have your folks been notified?''

Dumbly, numbly, Lou Ann shook her head. "I just couldn't bear to call them and tell them. I just *couldn't!*'' Her voice rose as she burst into hysterical sobs. Between spasms of crying her words came brokenly. "Doctor Kellerman, I know it was silly of me, but I just kept hoping—you know, hoping! I mean, that there was some mistake. That this was all just a bad dream. It—things like this don't happen to people like us! And I just couldn't bear to call Mother and Daddy and tell them that David's out there, dead in the snow—David, my brother!''

"I'll call your folks, honey," said the doctor. And all the time Rose was vacillating between the idea that the doctor was acting, that he had pulled that trigger himself, that he had killed once and would kill again in order to get what he wanted from the property—whatever it was—and thankfulness for his tender care.

They had planned to try to retrace Leslie's actions of the day before in order to come up with some clue as to why she had disappeared. And now she was probably dead. David was dead. It would be easy for a person to kill the second time. There was no doubt in her mind that he had killed Leslie—whoever he was—that the shot that had ended David Dedrick's young life had been an almost automatic thing. The pills the doctor had given her were already giving her some small relief. Mrs. Hanson was holding a cup of coffee in front of her and she was tempted to sit up.

"Go ahead and sit up, Rose," said Doctor Kellerman. "It won't hurt you. Drink the coffee. Probably be the best thing in the world for you." Turning to Lou Ann, he told her he'd go call her parents.

"Where's Allan?" asked Rose. Mrs. Hanson was sitting close to her.

"He went with the police," the other woman answered. "To see what's in the remains of the old burned out house. And to temporarily identify the body."

"It's David," said Lou Ann. "I'm sure of it. I'd

212

know him, if anyone would. I could even see that crazy beard."

"Positive identification will have to be made, anyway," said the doctor as he headed toward the door. "Of course, later. Hmmm, I wonder if the County Coronor has been called. Well, I imagine Larry Banks thought of that before he left the police station. Here they come now."

Tramping feet sounded on frozen ground. A draft chilled the room as the back door was opened. Subdued voices came from the vicinity of the kitchen. Allan Holliday came into the room with the lieutenant and the sergeant. He went directly to Rose. His face was ashen. "Are you all right?"

"Much better," she said. She noticed how his clothing made a cold breeze as he left her side and crossed the room to where Lou Ann sat staring dully into space. Then she listened to what he said and thought surely she had misunderstood him. Her mind must be playing tricks on her.

Lou Ann Dedrick apparently had not been able to grasp what he had said either. "What did you say?"

"I said that isn't your brother. The dead man. It isn't David."

"But it is! I saw him with my own eyes! I saw his hair and his beard and . . . it was my brother, I tell you!" Uncontrolled tears flowed again.

"No," Allan said quietly. The two officers were standing in the middle of the room. "That man is not David Dedrick. He's quite a few years older, and his hair is longer and his beard heavier. I thought at first glance that it was David, too. But then, I was prepared to see David. Just as you were. And you didn't turn him over to take a good look at his face. I could tell, because he was still face down in the snow."

"You told me not to," said the girl.

"Because I knew the police wouldn't want his body disturbed. He's still in the same position, but I got down on my knees and watched while the officers shone the light in his face. His features are nothing at all like David's, Lou Ann."

"I don't understand. Then who is it?" The girl sounded dazed. Her voice was high and thin, as if she were barely holding into herself. "Mr. Holliday, I know this sounds horrid, but I don't really care who it is as long as it isn't David!" The precarious hold she had on herself dissolved into a flood of relieved tears and Rose found herself getting to her feet, heading toward the young girl.

"Now you stay right there, Mrs. Winters. I'll attend to her." Mrs. Hanson spoke with authority. She put her ample arms around the girl and led her upstairs where she would have a chance to pull herself together.

"What else did you find out there?" Rose's voice was shrill.

"Nothing," said Larry Banks. "Just the dead man and a bunch of footprints in the snow that mill around and cross and recross each other."

"But in the basement of the burned house?" Her voice broke as she asked the question.

Allan came and sat on the couch. He put a protective arm around Rose's shoulders.

"We think your niece might be all right, Mrs. Winters," said Larry Banks. "Someone has been living in the basement of the old Overstock place for what appears to be several days. It's good and warm down there because of the hot springs. We could see where someone had built a fire, probably for cooking, and there were some opened cans of soup, some canned baked beans and some Spam as well as bread and butter and a little fruit. There was also a sleeping bag—and this." He held up a small silver object. "I rather imagine this belongs to your niece."

"Yes. It's Leslie's. She'd recently had her ears pierced, and she wore those little silver earrings all the time. Sometimes she had difficulty in getting them back in her ears when she took them out to clean them."

"It was on the sleeping bag, Mrs. Winters, along with some plastic clothes line. We think the girl was taken and held against her will down there in that old basement. The plastic clothesline had been recently cut."

"But she wasn't there?" Rose was bewildered.

"No," said Allan. "The lieutenant has a theory that David and Leslie might be in the tunnel. It's quite possible that David shot the other man. Don't forget that David has lived around here for a long time. He was the one who went running toward the ruin of the other house on top of the ground while Jim Hanson and I went down in the tunnel. We naturally assumed that it was David who was shot. All right, then he must have gone into the basement, found Leslie and untied her. It might seem the most natural thing for him to attempt to bring your niece back through the tunnel."

"Then why don't you go down there and see?"

"We've already tried that, Mrs. Winters. But the tunnel has caved in."

XVII

It seemed impossible, but only three days and nights had gone by since Rose had become uneasy about Leslie making it home safely in the blizzard. And it had been just that morning when she had heard Allan Holliday say in that chilling voice of doom that the tunnel had caved in. She hoped fervently that she would never be forced to live through another such harrowing experience. If anyone had told her at eight o'clock that morning that she would be sitting down to a meal with Leslie and David and her sister Irene and Allan Holliday, and looking forward to eating with a hearty appetite, she would have been amazed.

Mrs. Hanson had taken out her excess of nervous energy in a cooking spree that resulted in a magnificent feast. A baked ham was studded with cloves, and whole frozen strawberries nestled in a garnish of mint leaves. Baked sweet potatoes were in a blue bowl. Asparagus in a creamy cheese sauce steamed in an oval white one. Mounds of freshly baked

Parker House rolls sent up their crusty good fragrance. The sound of the percolator came from the kitchen and Allan Holliday carefully removed the cork from a bottle of champagne and poured ceremoniously. "To your continued good health," he said with a nod of his head to Rose. Then his face broke into a wide grin as he added, "And to your continued good luck, Leslie."

Leslie laughed. "I'll drink to Aunt Rose's good health, and I'll be delighted to have everyone else drink to my good luck." She sobered. "And it was good luck—and determination—on David's part."

"I can't get over it," said Irene. "As long as I live, I'll never forget the way Rose sounded when she told me Leslie was gone. She's always been partial to Leslie, you know," she added with a smile in the direction of Allan.

Rose felt the shadow of the old envy coming to the surface as she thought, *Now wait a minute, Irene, you have a husband. Allan belongs to me.* She didn't say it out loud, though. Instead, she gave David Dedrick a fond look and said, "And to think I was feeling so dreadfully ashamed of myself for doing what I did about going into the tunnel. I thought I was responsible for your death." She had decided the beard and the long hair were all right, as long as they were on David.

"I don't feel quite right about having dinner without Doctor Kellerman," said Mrs. Hanson. "I mean, Mrs. Winters, he did say to go ahead and eat if he wasn't here by six-thirty, but just the same, it doesn't seem right."

"I'm here!" The doctor came bustling in from the kitchen and took the empty seat at the table. "Babies, as I've said before, I'm sure, decide to be born at all hours, day or night. I just delivered an eight-pound boy in Washoe Valley, without benefit of a hospital. There wasn't time. My, this looks delicious." He reached for his wine glass and held it toward Allan. "I shouldn't drink with you, you scoundrel. It's pretty obvious that I'm out of the running as far as courting Rose is concerned. Oh well, may the best man win. I might still have a chance at buying this old house." He beamed. "I looked for a while as if I would have to marry the girl in order to get her property."

"She isn't selling," said Allan. "I'm going to move in with her. I always wanted to marry a rich widow with an expensive piece of property."

"Anyway," said Rose indignantly, "I already told you I wasn't interested in getting married again."

"You and this photographer going to live in sin?" The doctor speared a piece of ham and looked at it appreciatively. As he cut into it, he said he didn't care if anybody else was going to eat or not, he was starved. "And while I'm eating, perhaps some of you people will fill me in on exactly what happened. All I've got so far are dibs and dabs and not much of those. When they called me about that wreck out on 395 and I had to leave here, I understood that the tunnel had caved in and Leslie and David were trapped in there somewhere. I've been worried half out of my mind all day long. How about some of those sweet potatoes, Leslie, my girl?"

"It was Phillip Tremont, doctor, if you haven't heard." Irene's voice quivered with emotion. "Something told me right from the beginning that Phillip was behind Leslie's disappearance. He was quite mad, you know."

"Who the devil is Phillip Tremont?" Doctor

Kellerman's eyes looked from one person to the other. "I'm afraid I was suspicious of the wrong person. But who is this Tremont?"

"I was engaged to be married to him," said Leslie. "Except that just before the wedding he sort of let me know he already had a wife—and two children." Her face darkened. "I didn't even tell Mother this, but Phillip didn't see any reason why I shouldn't become his common-law wife."

"One of those hippies, huh?" The doctor helped himself to the asparagus. "I always said these young people with their long hair and beards are all crackpots. Except you, David. I've known you all your life. You're different. You'll outgrow it."

"Phillip didn't even have a beard until just recently," said Leslie. "As a matter of fact, he was straight arrow in nearly every respect. That's why my father liked him so much. They share—shared—the same point of view on politics and all the problems of the world."

"Oh, well, he couldn't have been all bad," the doctor said. "He probably had a good up-bringing and just went wrong somewhere along the line."

"He certainly did," said Leslie, "and he went even more wrong after I broke off with him. He said he would go through with the wedding, but of course it would make a bigamist out of him while a common-law marriage would not. It was just *too much*. I didn't tell my parents, but he kept hanging around bugging me all the time after he told me about his wife and children and I told him to get lost. That's why I decided to come to Carson City and go to work. I didn't think he'd find me there."

"You should have told your father and me," said Irene. "We could have done something."

"I just thought it would be easier this way.
never dreamed he'd find me. I felt that if I left tow
he'd forget about me. I guess nobody understand
how crazy someone can be until it's too late. H
asked a girl friend where I was. She told him. It wa
just that simple."

"Then he called here," said Rose, "trying to fin
out if she were here. I lied and said she wasn't, bu
he found out she really was."

"So he followed me here. The crazy fool. Boy, wa
I scared!" Scared or not, Leslie was digging into he
meal as if she were starved.

"What I never did get straight, Leslie, was th
information you stumbled across. When you calle
David and told him your life might be in danger.
Allan Holliday was looking at her intently.

"It was at the garage where I went to get my ca
The mechanic told me somebody had done som
thing to it to make it not start. Of course at tha
time I didn't know it was Phillip who had done it;
just figured it was somebody who for some reason c
other wanted this house desperately enough to d
anything. Like kidnap me and hold me for ranson
maybe. So I made a lot of telephone calls to th
county courthouse. I couldn't find anything tha
was recorded that might give a hint as to wh
anyone would want it. By the way, Doctor Kelle
man, why did you want to buy this place? Or do yo
still want it, really?"

"I'll tell you later. It has nothing to do with wha
happened. Right now I just want you to tell m
where you were and how you managed to disappea
from the place so quickly." He chuckled. "I'd als
like to know how you managed to keep from freezin
to death."

"Okay. I went to a dress shop on my lunch hour and bought a new purse and some other things, after I'd talked to the people about my car. Just as I was coming out, I saw Phillip. That is, I thought it was Phillip, but I wasn't absolutely sure. It upset me. I didn't want him to see me, so I went back into the dress shop and waited around until I thought it would be safe to go back to work. Well, I was late getting back from lunch because of that, but it was okay. I didn't have a lot on my desk. So I got to thinking about that house in San Francisco that Mother inherited. It was built by the wife of the man who built this house, after he died. During the time that Phillip and I were seeing a lot of each other, I'd told him about her diary. I didn't show it to him, but I did tell him that her husband had drowned and she hadn't seemed to be very upset by the incident—and I remembered something he said at the time. Maybe I wouldn't have given it a thought if it hadn't been for the weird things that had been happening around here. What he said was that he bet Becky Overstock was having an affair with Thurston, her husband's brother, probably even before old Peter Overstock died. It was such a little thing for me to remember, but I couldn't get it off my mind."

"There never was a breath of scandal as long as she lived in these parts," Doctor Kellerman said with conviction. "I understand she lived a rather interesting and unusual life in San Francisco after Peter Overstock died, but I doubt that she had anything to do with Thurston. I think if there was any gossip, even the slightest bit of evidence to fan the flames, the old time residents would have perpetuated it."

"What's important is that Leslie kept in mind

that conversation she'd had with Phillip," said Allan Holliday.

"Not really, but it made me a little wary, because it made me remember that Phillip knew about Virginia City and Aunt Rose's house. I thought it was a little far-fetched at first, for me to think Phillip was behind the haunting of the house, but after I saw him—well! Then I looked out the window and I saw him in his own car. Then I was sure it was Phillip. He was sitting in the parking lot, just three spaces over from where I'd parked on the night of the storm. That was when I called David."

"Why didn't you tell me everything?" David reached for her hand and squeezed it.

"Because it sounded so silly! Besides, someone came into the office just then and I had to get to work."

"But you could have called me back," David insisted. "Or you could have gone to the police."

"Look, I didn't know he was *that* crazy!" Leslie's voice was defensive. "I mean, after all, when you've known somebody for quite some time, it's a little difficult for you to anticipate something like the events that followed. How was I to know I was correct in my assumptions? Besides, I didn't really have anything to go on. Just a feeling of uneasiness, really. And I didn't want to see Phillip again. I had no idea he was going to do what he did. I just wondered if he had messed up my car."

"But you said your life might be in danger," David insisted.

"Well, I thought I could say that to you without making myself look ridiculous. And I thought I had enough time. After all, we were going to dinner that night. I had no idea he was going to be in the house when I got there."

"He was actually here?" Rose realized she had been sitting on the very edge of her chair. Most of the events that took place had already been talked out, but in the telling of things Leslie had understandably rushed along and run on ahead of herself some of the time.

"Yes. Only I didn't know it. I was congratulating myself on the fact that he hadn't hung around in the parking lot, waiting for me to come out. I just drove blithely home, said a few words to Mrs. Hanson and started to get ready to go out. I was in the bathtub when the lights went out. I thought I'd die of fright! Then when I started to get out of the tub the door opened and there he stood. With a blanket. He threw it over my head and at the same time wrapped it around my arms so I couldn't fight very well. It was a little like a straight jacket. He kept his hand over my mouth. I could hear Mrs. Hanson coming up the front steps and he carried me down the back steps. I think he was just barely out of the hall with me when she arrived on the landing. Of course it was very dark, so she probably wouldn't have seen us, even if we had still been in the hall."

"How did he get into the house without anybody knowing it?" Rose asked it, and Mrs. Hanson, who had come in with the coffee said she wasn't clear on that point, either.

"Through the tunnel. And with a skeleton key to the back door."

"You mean the trap door in the yard?" asked David.

"No. There's another opening. It's a natural cave-in, really. You see, Phillip had been living in the basement of the other house for about three weeks. He'd had plenty of time to explore the area. He also spent a lot of time in the libraries and museums, reading up on the Overstock family. But getting back to this natural opening: It's in the back of the house, just under the sidewalk by the kitchen windows. He'd found a turning place in the tunnel where they'd started to dig it out, but it looked as if they'd changed their mind. It was behind the stairs that led into the tunnel itself. He didn't have to do much digging to make a hole big enough for him to slip through. Then he was always very careful to cover the surface with rocks and dirt after he lowered himself back down there. Lately, of course, all he had to do was fluff up the snow. Unless you just happened to walk along the edge of the sidewalk, in which case you might stumble and fall, you would never dream the opening was there."

"Then he never used the trap door at all," said Rose. "It took me forever to open it, but of course it was frozen to the ground. I don't quite see where this opening is, though."

"It's under the sidewalk. There's just enough space on the edge for a person to slip through. That's where he shoved me! And he kept giggling all the while."

"Why in the world didn't you scream?" asked Mary Hanson.

"Oh, well, I'm getting ahead of the story. He took me down to the basement. I didn't have a chance to scream because he kept his hand over my mouth and he was pinching my nose. And giggling. Oh, it was awful! I could hear Mrs. Hanson thumping around upstairs, opening doors and calling my name, and there I was absolutely immobile. He waited until she had gone out of the house, and then he wrapped a gag around my nose and mouth."

"Didn't you try to get away from him?" David was looking at her miserably. "I can't understand how he could have done it unless you cooperated with him a little. After all, you aren't a little fragile girl so weak and frail that you couldn't have gotten in a few healthy kicks."

"David, he had a knife at my back. I could feel it. You just don't argue with a sharp knife. Besides, by then I knew he was stark raving mad. Just that continuous insane giggle was enough to let me know that."

Rose asked if that was when she dropped her class ring. She was thinking of the horror they had all experienced when they thought Leslie might have been put into the furnace.

Leslie drew a shaky breath. "I get terrified all over again when I talk about it. Yes. I reached for a tissue just as I was about to get out of the tub after the lights went out. I didn't think he knew about the tissue. Actually, I was groping in the dark for a towel, but my hands came into contact with the box of Kleenex on the shelf first, and my hands were wet and one came out of the box and stuck to my fingers. I didn't even think about it, either. I just kept it in my hand, all wadded up. It was while he was putting the gag on me that I slipped the ring off my hand and wrapped it in the tissue. I wasn't sure it dropped to the floor, either. I hoped it did, but for all I knew it was still hanging around somewhere in the folds of that awful wool blanket. It smelled to high heaven!"

"Then he took you upstairs and shoved you down

the opening by the sidewalk?" asked Allan Holliday.

"Yes. And let me tell you, that was the most horrifying moment of all. I didn't know how far I'd drop. I had visions of dropping several feet, thinking it was an abandoned mine shaft. I fell to the ground and sort of scrabbled around against the dirt and debris and I could hear him up above my head cramming things into the opening. Then he picked me up and pushed me, pulled me, dragged me, more or less, out of that little narrow place. After all, we were in the tunnel. And he started talking to me, telling me how easy it was to get a skeleton key that would open the back door. Aunt Rose, you simply *must* get some newer type locks that can't be opened with a skeleton key. Or a plastic credit card, either."

Leslie's mother shook her head. "I don't see how you can remember all of it. I'm sure I'd have fainted dead away. You poor child!"

Doctor Kellerman wanted to know what Phillip had said.

"Just crazy things. Like how he was going to talk some sense into my head. Sense into *my* head! It was dark in there, but he seemed to know his way around. I kept thinking of scorpions and black widow spiders and bats and things and there were some scurrying noises, but he kept pushing me when I'd begin to shake with fright, and stick that knife into my back. I found out later that he had a flashlight. But he said he was conserving the batteries for an emergency. When I heard water trickling in the absolute darkness, he turned the light on and showed me the snake all coiled up."

"Did he threaten you with the snake?" asked Irene.

226

"Oh, no. He just wanted me to be sure and step over it." Leslie looked down at her plate. "He kept talking about how I was the reincarnation of Becky Overstock and he was Thurston. He was sure they had a love affair. Said he'd read in the library where Becky was Thurston's girl in the first place, but Peter took her away from him. Oh, it was a far-out conversation, all right. All one-sided, of course. I couldn't say a word through that awful gag.

"Then there was a place where the steam was hissing through a break in the earth. He said it was all right, he'd been there before and it would only last for a little while and then we'd be in a nice warm place where he'd let me rest. Almost immediately after we got through the hot steamy place, we were in what looked like a basement. He let me lie down on a sleeping bag, but he didn't take the gag off because he said I might scream and he was sure I'd see things his way after he'd explained. He also said if I screamed somebody would probably hear me, then he'd have to kill me. He said it almost in the same way somebody else might say if you step in the cold water you'll get your feet cold and wet."

"All those hours, at the mercy of a madman!" Irene exclaimed.

"Well, I never gave up hope, Mother. I never once felt that I wouldn't get out of it alive. After all, I knew where I was. I felt pretty confident that someone would think of the old house that had burned. I won't say I wasn't afraid, because I was, but I didn't really think he would kill me."

Doctor Kellerman said as a general rule people tend to believe there is hope. He had stopped eating. His cake waited on the plate while he listened raptly.

"Oh, he said so much," Leslie went on, "it's hard to remember all of it. One thing was that he didn't really have a wife and two children. He said he'd just been teasing me, to make sure I was a nice girl, with moral values. Of course I didn't know whether to believe that or not. Along about then, I wasn't sure of much of anything.

"Then he started the haranguing. He really wanted me to see his point of view. That I am the reincarnation of Becky Overstock. I don't know whether that was something he dreamed up before he started reading all that old lore or whether he decided it afterwards. He had a picture of her that he'd torn out of a page in a museum. Actually, I do look a little like her."

"But so many people bear a resemblance to other people," Rose said.

"Oh, Phillip was convinced. He talked all night long. At least I thought it was all night long. Sometimes he'd leave me for a while and go out into the night. When he did that, he'd tie me up with some plastic clothesline. Then he'd come back and start in again. He wanted me to go along with him in his great scheme, in order to live the life he was convinced we both deserved. Aunt Rose's house was there, and what he wanted me to do was to kill you, Aunt Rose. Then we could live together in the house just as he felt we were supposed to do. He was sure that Peter had managed to take me (when I was Becky) away from Thurston, and since he was Thurston, we should be together in Peter's house. After all, Thurston's house was no longer there.

"Then he started in on this business that we had to figure out a way to kill Aunt Rose so I wouldn't be suspected. He knew David and Allan were sleeping at the house. He didn't trust either one of them. He was afraid they might get up and prowl around during the night and find the secret entrance to the tunnel. That was why he kept leaving me all the time. The last time, he came freaking back from outside and disappeared into the place where the steam was. When he came back he was giggling harder than ever. He said, 'I've just taken care of your Aunt Rose, baby. We don't have to worry about her.' Oh, I just knew he'd killed you, Aunt Rose!''

"He must have seen you when you were going down into the tunnel, darling." Allan shuddered as he looked at Rose.

Leslie said, "All I know is that he came back out of that tunnel madder than ever. After he told me he'd taken care of Aunt Rose, he said we'd have to go someplace where it was safe. He started to untie me when he heard footsteps ringing overhead. Then he said, in a rather offhand manner, that he guessed he'd have to kill everybody. He had a gun."

"Yeah, and I saw the gun glint in what little light there was when he came crawling out of that hole," said David.

"What hole?" Doctor Kellerman wanted to know.

"Where the steps had once been that led from the basement. I waited until he got out in the open, then I jumped him."

"Then you yelled," said Mary Hanson. "We all heard you."

"Damn right I yelled. He also had a knife. He cut this gash in my arm." David held up his left arm and showed a thick bandage. "Then I don't know how it happened, but I got his gun away from him and it went off. I thought I'd shot myself at first. Then I

229

panicked."

"I don't think you did so badly, David." Leslie's eyes were starry. "He came right to me, just as if he knew I'd be there."

"I did know you'd be there, Leslie. It was the only place you could be. Only I shouldn't have done what I did. I should have brought you right to the house."

"Yes. Why didn't you?" Leslie's mother leaned forward. "Poor Rose was absolutely frantic when I arrived. She was sure you and Leslie were down there underground, buried under tones of rock."

"I didn't take her straight to the house because I didn't know who the devil that fellow was." David's eyes turned to Allan Holliday. "I was thinking all along that you were in back of everything, sir. Of course I knew you were with Rose when Leslie disappeared, but I kept thinking you had someone working with you. I thought you'd found out there was an untapped lode of silver on the place or something. Then I was thinking about Doctor Kellerman along those lines, too. And there was Mitch LeBlanc to consider. I just didn't think it was safe to take Leslie back there to the house."

"You could have asked her while you were untying her," Rose pointed out.

"I told you I panicked. I didn't even notice that gag around her face. My fingers were shaking so hard I thought I'd never get that clothesline untied from around her arms and legs. Then I had to get her out of there. We went to a cave where I used to play when I was a child."

"And all that time I couldn't say a word," said Leslie with a laugh. "I kept making noises out of my nose, but David didn't notice. I remember thinking

230

I could just as well have been somebody else for all he knew. He didn't once glance at my face."

"I would have known those legs of yours anywhere," said David. "She was lying on her back on a sleeping bag, with that moldy old blanket wrapped around her. We must have made a ghostly looking pair snaking around the foothills to get to that cave."

"Then when we got there, he finally noticed that I wasn't saying anything."

"You should have noticed that right away, David," said the doctor. "When a woman doesn't talk all the time, there's bound to be a reason." He remembered his cake and started to cut into it with relish.

"It was getting near daylight by then," Leslie said, "and I saw the cut in David's arm. I was afraid he'd bleed to death before we could get it taken care of. By then he understood that Doctor Kellerman was to be trusted, but he knows a young medical student who lives a few yards from the cave where he'd taken me. We went there and then we came back here."

"Just in time to keep the police from alerting the whole area and starting rescue operations," said Allan. "As you know, Doctor, the tunnel is no longer in existence, except for a few feet. The cave-in almost obliterated it. Now will you tell us why you were so interested in this property? I must confess that you were my favorite suspect."

"Certainly," said the doctor. "The place is haunted. I belong to the National Foundation for Psychic Research. It's been haunted for years."

Leslie laughed. "You mean that business about

231

the lights going out and an unearthly voice calling for Becky? Phillip did that. He explained to me just how he did it. Through the cold air return ducts that lead from the furnace. He also did a number on the lights by using something he said he invented, called an interrupter. Well, I don't know whether it was really his invention or not, but it certainly did the trick."

"At least that's much nicer than killing me," Rose said.

"I guess I'd better tell you about the roses, Aunt Rose. I couldn't believe it was real when I saw those roses in the snow."

Rose Winters gasped. "*You* saw them, *too?*"

"I didn't know *you'd* seen them until Phillip spilled it all. I hesitated to tell anyone because it would have sounded like I was crazy."

"Yes, I saw them, and was sure no one would believe I'd seen any winter roses, either. They were there, and then they were gone."

"I know. They were theatrical stuff. Magicians' props. They're made out of stuff that self destructs within seconds of contact with moisture and air. He shot them with a sort of air gun, from the attic window. He bragged about his cleverness, then about his markmanship."

"Good heavens!" Rose shook her head. "That's just too much, Leslie."

The doctor cleared his throat importantly. "Well, that doesn't matter," he said. "That young man did his dirty work only recently. This voice has been heard off and on for years. That's why nobody would live in the house until Rose Winters came. Didn't you ever wonder why you couldn't rent the place, Rose?"

"I just thought it was too much work for a prospective tenant to consider. I mean, just getting rid of the accumulation of dirt and dust."

"No. The place is definitely haunted." The doctor smiled complacently.

"I told you, I told you time and time again, Mrs. Winters," said Mary Hanson. "You just wouldn't pay a bit of attention to me. Everyone around here knows about the ghost of Peter Overstock."

Rose Winters' lips were set in a grim line. In a measured voice she said, "*I don't believe in ghosts.*"

XVIII

There would be an inquest, of course, into the death
of Phillip Tremont. And it would take David a long
time to recover from the knowledge that he had
taken the life of another human being, even though
it was in self defense. Rose and Allan and Irene
talked about that after David and Leslie went out.
They also talked about the resilience of youth. Rose
was sure she would have spent the rest of the day in
bed, had she been Leslie or David, but Irene said it
was natural for them to want to get away from the
house and the older people. Doctor Kellerman left at
the same time Mrs. Hanson went to the cottage to
attend to Jim, who was not going to be up and
around for a while. His parting words had been
delivered with a mocking smile. "Don't be surprised
if some night the lights go out and you hear the
voice of Peter Overstock calling for his wife."

"You'd better have a good alibi if it ever does
happen," said Rose with a smile.

Irene went to bed and left Allan and Rose all alone

n the living room. They had a lot to talk about, and
'or once Rose was pleased with the tact her sister
1ad shown. After Allan had officially asked her to
narry him and she had agreed, they talked of other
,hings. She learned all the things he wanted her to
<now about his past and she allowed herself to tell
1im what she thought he ought to know about
1erself. Then they got involved in a conversation
1bout the possibility of a real ghost. Again she reit-
erated that she didn't believe the house was haunted
1nd he agreed with her.

He said, "A lot of these legends get started out of
1 shred of truth and then they build and build. Some
of the old castles in England are said to be haunted
1nd they've proved to be an invaluable tourist
.ttraction."

"I'd rather just live here in peace," said Rose.

"We'll have to travel some of the time," he
ointed out. But he agreed he wouldn't want to turn
he house into a museum to show off a frustrated
pirit, even if there were such a thing.

The next morning Mrs. Hanson said maybe the
'host was finally quieted. She said maybe it had
omething to do with a second case of violent death
ccurring on the property. Irene went home to San
'rancisco but promised to come back for Rose's
edding.

The wedding took place two weeks later, with
tose in pale mauve and Irene as matron of honor in
heer beige. Leslie served as maid of honor. Her
ress was just a darker shade of mauve and she was
eautiful, but Allan said nobody could possibly be
s radiantly beautiful as the bride. Irene's husband
ave Rose away and Doctor Kellerman was Best
1an while David acted as usher. It had been orig-

inally planned as a small wedding in the living room of the house, but people kept thinking of others to invite and Mrs. Hanson finally opened all the doors to the first floor of the house, even the double doors that led to the library. Mrs. Dedrick, who played the organ at the Baptist Church in Reno, played the opening bars of the wedding march and Rose took her brother-in-law's extended arm for the trip down the wide staircase. She drew in her breath at the sight of the flower-bedecked rooms and all those people down there who had assembled for her wedding. Irene was already standing in front of the fireplace with Leslie, and Allan was walking slowly toward the minister. He turned his head and smiled at Rose just as she reached the bottom of the stairs. Vaguely, she was aware of Mitchell LeBlanc, who had brought his invalid wife. And she caught Doctor Kellerman's eye as she took her place.

Doctor Kellerman had told her, quite seriously, that he wished her all the happiness in the world. She was grateful. Mitchell had asked her, slyly, if she were sure Allan was not marrying her for her money. She was able to laugh and it wasn't forced. She hadn't even bothered to tell Mitch that Allan was independently wealthy, with property of his own that was worth much more than anything she owned.

In that little space of expectant silence while everyone waited for the wedding ceremony to begin, Rose caught her breath and allowed the memory of Mark to enter her thoughts. She thought she felt his approval in what she was about to do. She had loved him and he had loved her. There would always be a very special place in her heart for the man she had shared many wonderful years with. She had always

236

known there were many kinds of love, but she had not quite believed herself capable of loving another man in the same way she had loved Mark. Actually, she didn't love Allan in the same way. She had been a different person then. Unsure of herself, much younger and . . . just different. Mark had been outgoing and Allan was basically a shy person. She felt a tenderness for Allan Holliday that she had not experienced in her first love. It dawned on her that she had needed Mark Winters. That she had basked in the wonder of his protectiveness. She didn't feel protective toward Allan in the same way that a mother feels for her child, but she felt that Allan needed her as much as she needed him. What they felt for each other was mature and deeply moving, a glorious thing to experience. In an adult way, she understood that the new marriage might not have all the glitter of a first romance, but in a different way it would be wonderfully thrilling, marvelously rewarding. Some day, she knew she would tell Allan how she felt just before she promised to love and honor him for the rest of her life.

The minister lifted his head and smiled. "Dearly beloved, we are gathered here together to join—"

The lights flickered, dimmed and then went out. Only the big white tapers in back of the minister glowed. Rose supposed someone had switched off the lights and she was glad. Probably Mrs. Hanson, she thought with that part of her mind that was not occupied in feeling the solemn vows she was about to take.

After a slight hesitation, the minister's voice continued. " . . . this man and this woman in holy matrimony. The State of Nevada has vested in me the great privilege of . . ." The voice stopped speaking again as a cold blast of air came into the house and wafted through the open rooms. The candle flames were sent into a frenzied fluttering, then sputtered and went out. Then the hollow sounding, plaintive call came into the room. The words were carried on the wings of the icy wind that blew harder, colder. "Help me, Becky! Help me!"

Rose felt her knees turn to water as the chills ran up and down her spine. Behind her, she felt the movement of suddenly turned heads, the hushed, startled sound of several indrawn breaths. But Allan's hand was steady. It was warm and tender. His voice sounded, firm and normal in the darkness. "Please continue, Reverend Clark."

"I love you," he whispered as he reached into his pocket for matches. The rich sound of the minister's voice continued without further interruption.

FOR THE FINEST IN MYSTERY AND SUSPENSE, IT'S LEISURE'S
CRIME COURT SERIES

Make the Most of Your Leisure Time with
LEISURE BOOKS

Please send me the following titles:

Quantity	Book Number	Price
_____	_____	_____
_____	_____	_____
_____	_____	_____
_____	_____	_____
_____	_____	_____

If out of stock on any of the above titles, please send me the alternate title(s) listed below:

_____	_____	_____
_____	_____	_____
_____	_____	_____
_____	_____	_____

	Postage & Handling	_____
	Total Enclosed	$ _____

☐ Please send me a free catalog.

NAME _____
(please print)

ADDRESS _____

CITY _____ STATE _____ ZIP _____

Please include $1.00 shipping and handling for the first book ordered and 25¢ for each book thereafter in the same order. All orders are shipped within approximately 4 weeks via postal service book rate. PAYMENT MUST ACCOMPANY ALL ORDERS.*

*Canadian orders must be paid in US dollars payable through a New York banking facility.

Mail coupon to: **Dorchester Publishing Co., Inc.
6 East 39 Street, Suite 900
New York, NY 10016
Att: ORDER DEPT.**